er Books Weekly Reader Books Weekly R
ader Books Weekly Reader Books Weekly
Reader Books Weekly Reader Books Weekly
y Reader Books Weekly Reader Books Wee
kly Reader Books Weekly Reader Books We
ekly Reader Books Weekly Reader Books W
Weekly Reader Books Weekly Reader Books
s Weekly Reader Books Weekly Reader Bo
oks Weekly Reader Books Weekly Reader B
ooks Weekly Reader Books Weekly Reader
r Books Weekly Reader Books Weekly Read
er Books Weekly Reader Books Weekly Re
ader Books Weekly Reader Books Weekly R
Reader Books Weekly Reader Books Weekly
y Reader Books Weekly Reader Books Week
kly Reader Books Weekly Reader Books We
eekly Reader Books Weekly Reader Books W
ekly Reader Books Weekly Reader Books

The Adventures of a Two-Minute Werewolf

Weekly Reader Books presents

The Adventures of a Two-Minute Werewolf

by Gene DeWeese

Illustrated by Ronald Fritz

Doubleday & Company, Inc.
Garden City, New York
1983

This book is a presentation of
Weekly Reader Books.

Weekly Reader Books offers
book clubs for children from
preschool through junior high school.

For further information write to:
Weekly Reader Books
1250 Fairwood Ave.
Columbus, Ohio 43216

Library of Congress Cataloging in Publication Data

DeWeese, Gene.
The adventures of a two-minute werewolf.

Summary: Fourteen-year-old Walt, discovering in himself a tendency to turn into a werewolf, puts his talent to constructive use in thwarting the activities of a gang of burglars.

[1. Werewolves—Fiction. 2. Mystery and detective stories] I. Fritz, Ronald, ill.
II. Title.
PZ7.D522Ad 1983 [Fic]
ISBN: 0-385-17453-5
Library of Congress Catalog Card Number 82–45285

Printed in the United States of America
First Edition

For Tom Aylesworth, who persevered through not one but two committees for this one.

Contents

1

"It's Not Even a Full Moon Tonight"

I guess I really lucked out the first time I turned into a werewolf.

For one thing, it only lasted a couple of minutes. For another, the only person with me was Cindy Deardorf. Anybody else, especially any other girl, would've gone bananas in about three and a half microseconds, and I probably wouldn't have lasted much longer myself. I mean, turning into a werewolf, even if it is only for a minute or two, is not the most relaxing thing that can happen to a guy, especially if he's not expecting it.

Luckily, Cindy isn't your typical fourteen-year-old, which may be the biggest understatement I'll make for at least the next couple of hours. Oh, she *looks* typical enough, in a cute, brunette sort of way, and she wears the usual tight jeans and baggy sweaters. It's what's in her head that's a little strange, which was a darn good thing for me.

Anyway, the first time it happened was one Sunday night last August when Cindy and I were walking back from the Warrensville County Fair, which she had enjoyed a lot more than I had. We'd gone on a few of the rides, but mostly we'd spent the evening watching the stage show, a small-time rock group that calls itself the Sevastopol Simians, or SS for short. A couple of them are from a nearby town called Sevastopol, which is where that half of the name comes from. They're also loud and flashy, with smoke bombs and special effects and phony instruments to smash up. One guy, under cover of one of their smoke bombs, made a quick change into an ape suit while he played—and eventually ate—an electric bass, which is where the other half of the group's name comes from.

It was all pretty gross as far as I was concerned, but Cindy seemed to like it. She had even been singing along with them the few times they played something that had anything remotely resembling lyrics or a tune. She even sang off and on while we walked home, luckily nothing she had learned from the Simians. I do have to admit that she has a pretty good voice, certainly better than any of the Simians, and I wouldn't be surprised if someday she makes it big, really big, as a singer. Provided, of course, that she doesn't decide to take over the world instead.

But like I started to say before I got sidetracked, that was the first night this werewolf thing happened to me. Actually, Cindy noticed what was happening before I did. The first I knew anything about it was when she suddenly slowed down and made a funny noise. "Urk" is about as close as I can come, and for a second I thought she had decided to try out one of the Simians' songs. But when I stopped and looked back at her, I saw that her eyes and mouth were all pretty wide open, and she wasn't looking at all musical.

"Walt!" she said, swallowing loudly. "You've got hair all over your face!"

Self-consciously, I reached up to brush it back from my forehead, and I wondered why she had mentioned it. I mean, it just wasn't like her to be nitpicking about grooming, not like Dad, who's still holding out for the crew cut.

"I suppose I better get it cut before school starts," I started to say, but Cindy "urked" again.

And that's when I happened to look at my hand, and I realized why she was "urking." There was hair all over my hand, back and front. I blinked, but that didn't do any more good than Cindy's "urking." The hair was still there when the blink was over, maybe even longer and thicker than before.

"There's hair on my hand," I said. Brilliant.

"I know," Cindy said. "Your face is all covered, too."

Now she was starting to sound more interested than scared. Like I said, Cindy Deardorf isn't your average everyday girl, which, like I also said before, was a darn good thing for me. I never could've coped with all that hair and someone screaming, too.

I touched my face again, but I couldn't tell if the hair I felt was on my hand—paw?—or my face. And my nose—well, it *felt* sort of flat and cold, maybe even a little wet.

"This *is* a joke, isn't it, Walt?" Cindy asked. She was moving closer to me, squinting up at me in the glare of the streetlight a few yards away. "When I wasn't looking, you put on a mask and some hairy gloves? Right? Like that guy who ate his bass?"

All of a sudden she reached out and grabbed a handful of hair on my cheek and pulled. Hard.

I yelled and Cindy jerked back. But she still

had a handful of hair. It was dark brown, nothing like the light reddish stuff I normally have on my head, and it was stiff and bristly, like a scouring brush, instead of soft and halfway curly.

And my cheek hurt.

"It's real!" she said wonderingly.

About the same time Cindy said that, I realized that my yell had been more of a roar than a yell. I closed my mouth as tightly as I could and hoped that no more noises like that would come out. To tell the truth, I couldn't think of anything else to do, except maybe run. Or faint.

I didn't do either one, quite, and then Cindy was squinting at me again, only now she didn't have to look up as much as before. I'm normally nine or ten inches taller than Cindy's five feet even, but now I was barely eye-to-eye with her. I was just thinking about asking her if I was shrinking as well as getting hairy, but she started talking again before I had the chance.

"You *look* just like Lon Chaney in his Wolf Man outfit," she said thoughtfully. "What do you *feel* like?"

I tried to say "I don't know," but it came out all garbled and growly, and that's when I realized something else. When Lon Chaney, Jr., was in his

Wolf Man suit, he never had any dialogue, just lots of growls and snarls.

"How was that again?" Cindy asked, leaning closer to me.

"I can't talk," I tried to say, but since I couldn't talk, I couldn't say it. Of course.

"Are you trying to tell me something?" she asked. Maybe I was being hypersensitive, but she sounded like she was trying to talk to Lassie.

I shook my head up and down in a huge, furry nod.

"You can understand what I'm saying?" she asked.

I gave her another huge nod.

"Do you have any idea what's happened to you?"

"Apparently I'm turning into a werewolf," I tried to say, but all that came out were mumbles and growls, with maybe a small howl or two. Helplessly, I shook my head back and forth.

"Have you ever done anything like this before?" Cindy asked. She was starting to walk around me. Taking a tour of inspection, I guess.

I shook my head violently.

She completed her tour with a puzzled frown. Then she looked up at the starlit sky, what little wasn't blocked out either by the glare of the street-lights or by the trees that lined both sides of the street.

"It's not even a full moon tonight," she said, and then she looked at me again. "I don't suppose you have any idea how long you're going to stay this way, do you?" she asked matter-of-factly.

I shook my head again, tried a few more words that didn't work out, and gave up. Then Cindy was looking down the street behind me and grabbing my hand.

"Come on," she said. "Someone's coming, and you wouldn't want anyone to see you like this. Would you?"

I shook my head. I wasn't all that happy about seeing *myself* like this.

But then, as her hand tightened on mine and she started to pull, she stopped. For the first time since her initial "urks," she looked a little uncertain. Maybe it was because of all the fur on my hand, or the fact that my fingernails had turned pretty much to claws by now.

"You are still in there, aren't you, Walt?" she asked, peering at me even more closely, right into my eyes. "I mean, no matter what you look like on the outside, *you're* still inside there somewhere. Aren't you, Walt?"

I nodded and managed not to growl.

"Okay," she said, "then we'd better get you out of sight. Not everyone would take this as well as I did."

Another understatement, needless to say, but that's Cindy for you. Anyway, she got me away from the street and into an alley by the time the car she had seen came by.

But the alley, one of those residential ones with shrubs and garages and garbage cans on both sides, turned out to be a mistake. We hadn't gotten more than forty or fifty feet in when a pair of headlights flashed on and practically blinded us. I got one paw up in front of my furry face, and then the headlights started toward us with a roar.

By this time, the car out on the street had gone by, so we scrambled back to the sidewalk. We even managed to get through an opening in one of those big, shaggy hedges and into someone's front yard before the headlights came out of the alley after us.

And as I peeked back through the hedge, I recognized the car and realized how lucky we were that we weren't still out there on the sidewalk where we could be seen.

It was Stanley Olinger's '57 Plymouth with the big tail fins, and Stanley himself was leaning out

the window and trying to locate us with a spotlight mounted next to his outside mirror. He was sweeping the beam up and down the sidewalk like the spotlight in a prison-break movie.

I thought for a minute he was going to stop the car altogether and start looking for us on foot, but he didn't. Instead, I heard someone else in the car say something, and then Stanley muttered something back. I couldn't catch any of the words, but Stanley sounded really ticked off. And he switched off the spotlight and drove away.

I breathed—panted?—a huge sigh of relief. Stanley was sixteen and was going to be a junior this fall. He was also the closest thing Warrensville High had to organized crime. He and his two buddies, Tim Stratton and Willard Tucker, would shake you down for your lunch money or anything else they could get their hands on, and that was in broad daylight. Who knows what they would try in an alley at ten or eleven at night? I didn't even stop to think that, looking as hairy and fangy as I did, I might have a certain advantage, which just goes to show how brave and resourceful I am.

Anyway, it's just as well I didn't try to take advantage of my hairy state with Stanley right then, because that's when I started to change back. It was Cindy who noticed first again, since my mind was still occupied with stewing about Stanley. Besides, she was still holding my paw and probably felt it turning back into a hand.

"Walt!" she said, letting go of my paw/hand and standing back to get a better view. "You're coming back!"

Since we were behind a pretty thick hedge now, I wondered for a second if it could be the streetlights that had been making the change happen. I mean, werewolves are supposed to come out when there's a full moon, and those weird-looking lights they put up a couple years ago might look like a bunch of full moons to a werewolf that didn't know any better.

"Wow!" Cindy exclaimed. She seemed to have forgotten all about Stanley, and to tell the truth, I almost had, too. "*Where* is all that hair going? It's not falling off, it's just sort of—sort of crawling back in! And you were all hunched over, too, did you know that? But now you're straightening up again."

So that was why I'd been on eye level with her. I watched my hands, which were shaking, and pretty soon the hair was all gone except for the fuzz that grows there normally. I felt sort of itchy all over for a few seconds, but then even that stopped.

"Wow!" Cindy repeated. She just stood there looking at me, like she was waiting for my next trick. "I don't suppose you could do that again?"

2

"Maybe Your Folks Found You in a Field, Like Clark Kent"

"No!" I said sharply, now that I was finally able to talk again. "I *couldn't* do that again!"

At least I hope not, I added to myself.

"You're sure about that? I mean, if you could do something like that whenever you felt like it . . ."

Her voice trailed off, but her green eyes almost sparkled. She was starting to sound as if she'd just found a new toy and was trying to figure out what to do with it.

"Well, I can't," I said as firmly as I could manage. "And even if I could, I wouldn't."

Cindy did her best to look sympathetic, but she couldn't get all the sparkle out of her eyes.

"Yeah," she said finally. "I suppose it must be

a little rough on you, being inside there while all that's going on. What *is* it like?"

It wasn't really like anything, except for the itching there at the end, so I shrugged.

"Scary, that's all," I said.

She watched me another few seconds, but then she apparently decided I wasn't going to do anything else spectacular, and we started walking again.

"You never did that before?" she asked after half a block. "Never ever?"

I shook my head. "Never ever. I don't even *shave* yet."

"But why should it happen now?" she wanted to know. Then her eyes brightened as she looked up at me again. "Hey, you don't suppose it could've been that guy in the Simians, do you? Maybe he was real?"

"Don't be silly," I said. "That was just some guy in an ape suit! Besides, even if he was real, what would a weregorilla have to do with me being a were*wolf?*"

"If that's what you were. Anyway, don't ask me. You're the werewolf."

"Besides, I didn't get anywhere near the guy, so how could he have bitten me?"

"Who says they have to bite you?" She

shrugged as we walked. "But you're probably right. He did look pretty phony. One of his seams looked like it was coming loose, too. And *you* didn't have any seams. I could see that much, anyway."

She was silent for another half block, and then she said, thoughtfully, "If you want to know the truth, Walt, I think it probably happened because you've seen too many monster movies."

"Sure! Then why haven't *you* changed into something? You've seen as many as I have."

She shrugged again. "Who ever heard of a girl werewolf?"

"There've been a couple," I said, but then I couldn't think of the names of the movies. "Anyway, you could turn into something else, like a leopard. You've seen *Cat People* enough times."

"I'm just not as suggestible as you are, that's all. You know you're always doing things like that."

"Things like what?" I looked down at her as we walked.

"You know. Whenever anybody gets hurt, even in a movie, you get an imaginary pain in the same place."

"That's called empathy," I said.

At least that's what Mom had told me once.

She has a word for everything. But, then, I suppose she would. She's a writer, although you might get an argument about that from Dad. For Dad, a "writer" is someone who gets good reviews in the New York *Times*. Someone who turns out a paperback thriller every three or four months in her spare time is a "hack." Not that he really objects to her doing it, but he didn't object either when she said she'd use the name "Morgan Wilson," which is a combination of her grandfather's name and her grandmother's maiden name. She thought it sounded better than "Wilma Cribbens," which is her real name, and Dad thought it sounded safer for his "position at the bank."

"Sure it is," Cindy said. "It's also called 'letting your imagination run away with you.' Besides, I wouldn't be surprised if you hadn't been a werewolf for years. You probably just never noticed."

"Come on! How could I miss something like that? I mean, there was hair all over me! And I couldn't even talk!"

"You never do talk very much," she said. "And you *didn't* notice what was happening until I told you about the hair on your face."

"Maybe not. But I *would* have."

"Would you? You aren't the most observant person in the world, Walt Cribbens."

I tried to protest some more, but I was half afraid she might be right. Except for a little tickling, I hadn't really felt much of anything. And I was back to normal in a couple of minutes. I suppose, if I'd been by myself, or even sleeping . . .

"I still think I would've noticed," I said finally. "Besides, even if it has happened before, that doesn't explain *why* it happened."

"That's true," she admitted. "I don't suppose anyone else in your family does this sort of thing? What about your mother? She writes about werewolves and stuff like that all the time."

"Just once!" I said. "Just one werewolf in a dozen books, and that wasn't really a werewolf anyway. It was an alien shapechanger. You know that."

Cindy looked me over again. "You suppose *that's* what you are? You're from another planet and changing into a werewolf is normal for you?"

"Oh, come on!"

"No, really! Maybe your folks found you in a field, like Clark Kent. Or maybe *they're* aliens, too. I've always kind of wondered about your father, anyway. He always looks so *much* like a bank manager. I mean, if he really *was* a bank manager, he wouldn't look *that* much like one, not all the time."

I shook my head, trying to keep up with her ideas. "Look, even if I was a shapechanger, why should I change now? And into a werewolf, yet! And only for two minutes, for crying out loud!"

She shrugged. "Maybe it was a test run. Or maybe you're a two-minute werewolf. Or maybe back on your home planet, it's the time of the full moon. If your home planet has a moon. Hey!" she said, suddenly raising her voice and snapping her fingers. "Maybe *that's* it! Maybe your home planet is someplace like Mars. On Mars, they've got one moon that goes around so fast it rises in the west. And it's pretty small, too. Maybe your moon is too small and fast to change you for very long."

I shook my head, half afraid something would rattle. "Look, even if that made sense—which it doesn't—it wouldn't really explain anything. Why would a moon I can't even see make me change into a werewolf?"

"Why would a moon you *can* see make you change into one?"

"How should I know? Maybe it's—it's psychosomatic, like you said. Besides, it doesn't. Werewolves are just a legend."

"I guess that makes you a legend, then," Cindy said, grinning. She likes to play with words as much as Mom does. "A legend in your own time."

"You know what I mean! Werewolves aren't *real!*"

"Except for you?"

"But I wasn't a *real* werewolf. I mean, I didn't *feel* like one."

"So how does a 'real' werewolf feel?"

"Oh, you know! They always want to go out and kill people."

"Maybe that's just movie werewolves," she said. "And you know you can't believe everything you see in the movies. Maybe werewolves have the same problem regular wolves have. Regular wolves are really awfully nice, you know. They just get a lot of bad press. Maybe *were*wolves are nice, too. You certainly weren't all that bad."

"All right, maybe werewolves *are* nice, but none of this *explains* anything, for crying out loud!"

"Can't you ever take anything on faith, Walt Cribbens? I mean, I don't understand how electricity works, but I don't let that keep me from watching television."

"Huh?"

"Well, television uses electricity, doesn't it?"

"Sure, but what does that have to do with werewolves?"

"It's just that I take television on faith, that's all. Look, I even fixed your set once, remember?"

"No, you didn't! You just kicked it!"

"Well, it worked after I kicked it, didn't it? So I fixed it."

"Okay," I said finally, "you fixed it. But what does kicking a TV set have to do with my being a werewolf? You planning to kick me next time and hope that knocks the hair off?"

"Don't be silly. But it's simple, really. I don't understand television any more than I understand werewolves. They're *both* magic as far as I'm concerned." She shrugged. "Come to think of it, maybe it was that magician we saw at the Bijou a couple months ago that started it."

"He wasn't a magician," I explained, "he was a hypnotist."

"Well, whatever he was, maybe he got you started. Remember all those people he had up on the stage? All acting like Great Danes and Abominable Snowmen and weather balloons and things?"

"But *I* wasn't up there!"

"Maybe not, but you almost were. I saw you when he was talking to the audience and putting everyone under his spell. If I hadn't poked you, you would've been hypnotized right out of the audience."

She was right, I had to admit, at least to myself. I was just about ready to conk out when she had jammed her elbow halfway through my ribs.

"Probably a good thing I didn't let him get you up there," Cindy said. "If he'd told you to act like a Saint Bernard, you probably would've really changed into one, right there where everyone could see you."

"You really think—" I stopped and shook my head. "No, that's silly."

"Any sillier than what you did a few minutes ago?"

"I guess not," I admitted. "But darn it! I didn't *do* anything! Whatever happened, it was done *to* me. Anyway, I'm beginning to think we both just imagined the whole thing."

"Maybe *you* imagined it, but *I* didn't!"

"You're sure?" I asked. We had reached her house by now and were climbing the steps onto the front porch. "Maybe the light was bad, and—"

"Bad light makes you lose your voice and growl?"

"Well, no."

"It's up to you, I guess, whether you want to believe it happened or not." She shrugged and opened the door. "You want to come in? We've got some cherry pie left over from supper. Or don't werewolves eat cherry pie?"

"This one does," I said, but then I held back. "You're not going to tell anyone about this, are you? Especially not that ratty little brother of yours."

She shook her head. "Not unless you can put on a demonstration to back me up. Think you could do it again?"

"No!"

"Maybe later? When you've had a chance to rest up?"

"Not if I can help it!"

"I guess I won't tell anyone, then. Not right now, anyway, even if I do have proof."

"Proof? What proof?"

"Just this," she said, holding her hand out to me. "Here, you probably need it more than I do. Besides, it really belongs to you, anyway."

Then she dropped the little tuft of wiry brown werewolf hair in my hand and went inside without waiting to see if I followed.

I did, but not before I realized that my cheek was hurting again—and that I definitely had not heard the last of the werewolf business. If Cindy had anything to do with it—and I didn't see how I could keep her out of it—it was just the beginning.

3

"If It Worked at All, I'd Be a Wereduck"

The next day, Monday, was a very long day.

For one thing, I woke up at six o'clock and couldn't get back to sleep. Normally, these last couple of weeks before school starts, Mom indulges me and lets me sleep in as late as I like. As long as I fix my own breakfast, leave the kitchen pretty much the way I found it, and get to the golf course in time to do my caddying, she doesn't bug me much.

Therefore, as you can imagine, my coming into the kitchen about the time she was starting breakfast was considered just short of the Eighth Wonder of the World, or at least of Warrensville. Even Dad, who was just coming in from his daily, two-mile sweatathon, stopped panting long enough to widen his eyes and ask Mom who "this strange person" was.

Mom, of course, got into the spirit right away. "He *says* he's our son, but he doesn't have any ID."

"Well, all right," Dad said while he stood there melting before our eyes. "Take a chance and feed him this once. But keep an eye on him." With which he staggered the rest of the way to his shower.

Mom, who looks a lot trimmer and more athletic than Dad despite the fact that she never does anything much more strenuous than move her portable typewriter from room to room, made a small face as his severely sweating form disappeared down the hall. When he bugs her every so often to go jogging with him, she just says "Redheads don't have to exercise," which makes absolutely no sense at all and therefore drives him right up the wall.

"You're not sick, are you?" Mom asked as she went back to fixing breakfast.

I shook my head. "I'm okay. I just couldn't sleep."

"What time did you go to bed?"

"A little after eleven," I said. I didn't tell her that I hadn't been able to get to sleep until almost three.

"You have something big planned for today?"

"Just the usual. Doc Sheaffer wants me to caddy a couple rounds for him and Kingsley."

"They're the big tippers?"

"Pretty big."

She poked the sausages around the skillet and glanced at the clock over the refrigerator. Dad was due back in exactly ten minutes. Seven minutes to shower and three to dress. He always shaves before going jogging—he wants to look respectable in case he runs into any of the bank's customers on his rounds—so that chore was out of the way. And, with his crew cut, he doesn't have to waste any time combing his hair; he just makes sure it's standing up properly around the edges.

"Everything go all right at the fair last night?" she asked. "You didn't say much when you came in."

"Oh, sure, Mom, everything went swell."

"You and Cindy get to see that rock group she was talking about?"

I nodded, making a face. "More smoke and tricks than music."

"And nothing unusual happened?"

"What could happen?" I asked. She was still watching me, and I was getting more nervous all the time. I am definitely not the world's most accomplished poker face. Watergate would've lasted about twenty-seven seconds if I'd been involved.

"Anything you need from the library?" I asked, which was the best spur-of-the-moment distraction I could think of. "I think I'll go down there this morning. Before I go to the golf course."

"You're *volunteering* to run an errand? You *must* be sick."

"Come on, Mom!" I protested weakly.

She shrugged after a couple of silent seconds. "Well, far be it from me to inspect a gift horse's tonsils. And as a matter of fact, I just happen to have a half-dozen books you can return for me. They're due today, and I'm ten pages behind schedule on the rough draft of my latest masterpiece."

"Okay. Incidentally, what's this one about?"

"I'm not sure yet. That's one reason I'm behind schedule. I don't know where I'm going. I started out with some DNA experiments getting out of hand, but now I'm not so sure. It's turning into just another monster story."

She laughed as she poked some more at the sputtering sausage. "I'm tempted to make it into another shapechanger, but people might think I was repeating myself."

I didn't say anything. At the word "shapechanger," I more or less froze, naturally. I probably looked nervous and/or guilty, but she didn't seem to notice, and after a while I managed to get my mouth started again. With Mom doing most of the talking, we even managed to kick her plot around a fair amount, which she likes to do now and then. She says it helps her to think out loud, and Dad isn't much help. It's not that he's unimaginative or "disapproves" of what she writes or anything like that. It's just that he never reads "that kind of stuff," can't imagine why anyone else would, and therefore knows absolutely nothing about it. Sort of the way I feel about brussels sprouts.

Anyway, by the time Dad returned, I had pretty well gotten over my twitchiness and was munching on a sausage link, holding it in my fingers like a round, fried candy bar. He looked every bit as much like a banker as Cindy had said last night. He even had a vest on. A *gray* vest.

He gave my sausage link a sideways glance as he sat down and carefully unfolded a napkin.

"Yes," he said with a sigh, "I fear this must indeed be our son. Most others of his age have learned the proper use of knife and fork."

I finished the sausage with a fast gulp and hastily wiped my fingers on a napkin. I knew he wasn't *too* serious about his knife-and-fork crack, but things always went better if I didn't push my luck.

"I saw Sheriff Whittenberger this morning," he announced when Mom sat down with us.

I dropped my fork and was barely able to pick it up again. All that twitchiness I thought I'd gotten rid of was back, only worse. Despite the fact that it was impossible, I just *knew* that the sheriff had somehow or other found out I was a werewolf and he had told Dad. I figured Stanley Olinger, who just happens to be the sheriff's nephew despite his criminal tendencies, must have recognized me through all that hair last night in the alley and told his uncle.

Luckily, before I could blurt out either a confession or a denial, Dad explained his announcement, and it didn't have anything at all to do with me or a werewolf or even Stanley. Dad had just happened to run into Whittenberger and a deputy in front of Joe Olsen's house three or four blocks away, and, since Mr. Olsen works at the bank, Dad had stopped and marked time long enough to find out that Olsen's house had been burglarized the night before, while everyone in the family was at the fair. The burglars had gotten a couple of TV sets, a brand-new video recorder, and some jewelry.

I didn't contribute much to the conversation, and as soon as Dad left, I unchained my bike from the porch railing and started downtown. After a couple of blocks, I turned around and came back for Mom's books, which I had of course forgotten. She just looked at me. She was used to me forgetting things, so she didn't say anything, but her look was sort of suspicious. At least that's the way it looked to me, but in my state of mind, I'd probably think the stone lions around the courthouse were looking at me suspiciously. I even wondered for a second if Mom could possibly think that maybe *I* was the one who had broken into the Olsens' place just because I looked guilty and had been out of the house last night.

But she *couldn't* think *that,* I told myself as I took off on the bike for the second time. She just couldn't possibly think something as dumb as that. I mean, thinking I'd turned into a burglar last night was *almost* as dumb as thinking I'd turned into a werewolf . . .

Cindy and I hadn't made any plans to meet the night before, but she showed up at the library only a few minutes after I did. I guess we're both research-minded.

It didn't do us a lot of good, though. The Warrensville Public Library doesn't go in heavily for werewolf lore. Practically the only thing we found was a book on the children's side called *Werewolves and Other Monsters*. It was by someone called Aylesworth, and it wasn't all that helpful. Oh, it told us a couple of dozen ways you could be turned into a werewolf, but none of them were what you would call scientific or even practical. Mom's DNA experiments gone wrong made more sense, but Cindy wasn't easily discouraged.

"How about this?" she asked a few minutes later. After a quick skim, I'd given up on the book, but she was still digging through it.

I looked at the paragraph she'd been reading. I made a face.

"No," I said, "I don't think this is how it happened."

She moved on a paragraph. "Here's something else. Drinking water from a wolf's footprint." She scrunched her face up. "Sounds pretty yucky. You never did anything like that, did you?"

"Hardly. I've never even *seen* a wolf outside a zoo."

"You don't have to see one. All you have to do is see a footprint."

I shook my head.

"What about that cereal bowl you used to have when you were a little kid?" she asked.

I blinked. "Cereal bowl?"

"You know. That thing with the animal's picture in the bottom."

"Come on! That was a duck, not a wolf. Or a mouse, maybe. Besides where does it say in that book that eating out of a cereal bowl will turn you into *anything?*"

"It doesn't, but they probably didn't *have* cereal bowls with animals in them back then, that's all. You probably found a new, modern way of doing it."

"I told you, it wasn't even a wolf in the bowl. If it worked at all, I'd be a were*duck*. Or a were-mouse, maybe."

"Or a were-cornflake," she said and then went back to paging through the book. I guess I was lucky she didn't make any cracks about how I was already pretty corny and/or flaky.

A minute later, she found something else. "This one looks even better," she said, pointing to a page.

I leaned over her shoulder to read. People in Italy, this page said, believed people became werewolves if they had been born at the time of a new moon.

"But that's even dumber than cereals bowls. There's a new moon every month, for crying out

loud! If it worked that way, we'd be up to our ears in werewolves."

"Maybe we are. If they're all as quiet about it as you are, no one would ever know. Why don't you check with your mother?"

"Sure! I can just imagine me going up to her and—"

"I'll ask her if you want me to."

"I don't!"

"How'll you ever learn anything if you don't ask questions?"

"Just never mind, all right? Besides, this is all dumb, anyway. Look at all those pictures. I'm not even the same kind of werewolf as these. These all look like regular wolves."

"Aha! I *told* you it was because you'd seen too many monster movies!"

"What?"

"You look like a movie werewolf, not a real one, like these. So it has to have something to do with werewolf movies, not real werewolves. See?"

And that's the way it went. I hadn't expected to find anything helpful in the library, and I didn't.

I spent most of the afternoon caddying, but I had trouble keeping my mind on the job. As usual, I was carrying two bags, but I kept getting them mixed up and putting clubs in the wrong bags, not seeing where the ball went, setting the bags down with a clank just when someone was going into his backswing, that kind of thing. Needless to say, I didn't get as big a tip as usual.

And then, just to make the day really perfect, when I went around back of the clubhouse to where I had chained my bike to a tree, the bike wasn't there.

But Stanley Olinger was.

4

"Never Startle a Werewolf"

Maybe I should explain about Stanley. Like I said before, he's Sheriff Whittenberger's nephew, but that's just the start of the problem. For one thing, his uncle apparently believes everything Stanley says, and so do a lot of other people. The trouble is, Stanley doesn't look or act like your typical high school tough guy, at least not around his uncle or most other grown-ups. He gets good grades, too, and he's a natural-born actor. He'll probably graduate to corporate crime someday. When it comes down to your word against his, he always wins unless you happen to have a Polaroid shot of him doing whatever it is you accused him of doing, and even then he'll probably make most people believe you tricked him into it.

And if you so much as *try* to tell someone—like a teacher—about something he's done, you know he'll get you, somehow, somewhere. There are a couple of teachers who are on to him, I think, but even that doesn't help, the way his uncle sticks up for him.

And here I was, in back of the golf course clubhouse without so much as a witness, or even a whip and chair. Stanley was his usual immaculate self, almost as neat as Dad, which is one reason people believe *him* instead of *us,* since we're just your everyday, run-of-the-mill, sloppy teenagers. He looked like Lawrence Welk's grandson. Knit shirt with a little alligator on it. Dark slacks. Relatively short hair, not quite a crew cut. Regular shoes instead of sneakers. Like I said, Mr. Believability.

"You lose something?" he asked.

"It looks that way," I said.

"Something like this?" He held up the chain I'd last seen attaching my bike to the tree.

"That's part of it." I may have sounded calm, but I was mostly Jell-O beneath the surface. Furious Jell-O, but Jell-O nonetheless.

"Thought so." He clicked the lock shut, poked at it with a little metallic gadget that didn't look quite like a key. The lock popped open.

"Not much of a lock," he said. "You're lucky I happened by or you could have been out some *real* money."

So that's what he was up to. It was Stanley's version of the protection racket. He'd already pulled it with the lockers at school. Being paid not to break into them had kept him and his two buddies in spending money for at least the last year, but it looked like he was branching out, going into business for himself. I suppose he needed the extra money for gas now that he owned a car. I was still a little surprised that Tim and Willard weren't around.

Anyway, I gritted my teeth and got it over with as quickly as I could. He took a little less than half of what I'd made that afternoon and then showed me where he'd stashed my bike "for safekeeping." He also promised to "look after it" whenever I wanted him to in the future. I figured he was finished with me for the day when I got the bike back, but he wasn't. I was getting on and starting to pedal away when Stanley put a hand on the handlebars and brought me to a stop.

"One more thing," he said. "You and your girl friend were out a little late last night. I'd watch it, if I were you."

My filling of furious Jell-O turned to just plain

Jell-O in a second or so. He *had* seen us and recognized us, and he knew the truth about me and—

"I heard there were a couple burglaries last night," Stanley was going on when I started listening again. "Two people involved, according to my uncle, the sheriff." He paused, cocking his head sideways as he looked at me. "One of them could have been a girl."

Then he grinned and shrugged. "But I know it couldn't have been you two, so there's really no need to tell my uncle about seeing you last night, now is there?"

I was so relieved I almost fell over. All he'd really seen was Cindy. He hadn't seen me—or my then-furry face, at least—at all. He was just guessing that I was the one with her, since we were known to hang out a lot together. So all Stanley was doing was threatening to tell his uncle we'd been out late last night, which everyone knew anyway. I certainly wasn't going to fork over the rest of what I'd made today just to keep him from telling his uncle something that everyone already knew.

All of which just got me mad again. I jerked the handlebars out of his hand and headed around the clubhouse toward the road before he could recover and grab me.

"You can tell him anything you want to," I said. I didn't look back. Defying Stanley, even when you know you're right and don't have anything to lose, is easier if you don't have to face him, at least for me.

I knew that telling what had happened wouldn't do any good, so I just kept quiet about my loss. Besides, since it was getting on toward evening, I had other things to worry about. After supper, I stayed in my room most of the time, and when I was anywhere else in the house, I was ready to get back there quick if I noticed so much as one extra hair popping up where it didn't belong. I tried reading a collection of science fiction stories I'd gotten from the library last week, but that was a lost cause altogether.

I even tried listening to some folk music records Dad had gotten me for my birthday, but that didn't work much better than reading. Time went by at a rate of about one minute every hour and I heard maybe one note out of every hundred.

I made a dozen trips to the kitchen and ate probably a pound and a half of chocolate chip cookies out of sheer nervousness, and I ended up watching reruns on TV, which I hadn't liked even when they were new. Luckily, Dad was out at a meeting of some kind, and Mom had gone back to her manuscript after supper, trying to get back on schedule, so my weird behavior didn't get as much attention as it could have. Still, I could tell Mom knew something was up, the way she looked at me every time I went past the open door of the little room she used for an office.

Then, around nine, Cindy called.

"Are you going to do it again?" she asked.

"How should I know?"

"If *you* don't know, who does? Look, I'll be right over to keep an eye on you," she said, hanging up almost before the last word was out.

She was at the front door in five minutes. Ten minutes later we were down in the basement rec room, making believe we were going to use Dad's one bad habit, his pool table. Mom looked surer than ever that something was going on that shouldn't be, but she didn't push it. In case Mom was listening more closely than usual, we knocked the balls around a lot, though we hardly ever got anything in a pocket. Mostly Cindy just waited and kept asking me how I felt every thirty seconds or so.

Around nine-thirty, I started itching.

"It's happening," I said.

Cindy dropped her cue stick and came around the table toward me. "I don't see anything," she said.

"So far it's just an itch," I said.

It must be like growing a beard, I thought. Uncle Jerry said his itched like crazy at first, but it quit when it got long enough.

"I can see it!" Cindy said in an excited whisper. Her eyes were popping.

A second later, she whipped a camera out of somewhere, one of those one-step, instant jobs, and foofed me in the face with a flash. Not once but a half-dozen times. She probably would've done it more if she hadn't run out of film.

I itched another few seconds, and it was over.

"It didn't last as long this time," Cindy said, sounding disappointed.

"How do you know?" I asked when I was able to talk again.

"It just seemed shorter. But next time I'll time it. I know where I can get a stopwatch."

"The least you could've done was warn me about those flashbulbs," I said. "That could be dangerous."

"Dangerous? How?"

"Never startle a werewolf. You never know how one might react."

"But it's *you.*"

"So far."

She was quiet a second, maybe even having a doubt or two. But then she looked down at the pictures lying helter-skelter on the pool table. The first ones were almost finished developing.

I looked at them.

Believe me, it was scary. Up until then, I'd been on the inside looking out. Well, the pictures put me "out front," so to speak, and gave me quite a jolt.

"You look more like Michael Landon than Lon Chaney," Cindy said. "You know, in *Teenage Werewolf.*"

I suppose she was right. After all, I *was* a teenage werewolf. But it didn't make a lot of difference. Landon and Chaney were both a lot hairier than I really cared to be.

"Are you going to tell your folks?" Cindy asked. "Now that we've got some proof . . ."

I started to say "Yes, at least Mom," but then I stopped. I *wanted* to tell her. If anyone would understand, she would. But what could she *do?* Call a doctor?

And what good could a doctor do, anyway? I mean, turning into a werewolf isn't in the same league with an upset stomach or even measles. As far as I know, nobody's developed a werewolf vaccine. And even if they had, it was too late for me. You have to be vaccinated *before* you contract the disease. After you've caught it, there's only rest and liquids and antibiotics.

Besides, she'd probably just have to tell Dad, and he would simply go bananas. He has enough trouble coping with life at the bank, or so he says when he's raiding the aspirin bottle. Having a werewolf for a son would send him off the deep end for sure.

And other people would probably find out, maybe even the newspaper. And once that got started, who knows where it would end? Television talk shows? The *National Enquirer*, for crying out loud? I'd thought now and then that it would be nice to be famous, but I didn't think that being a werewolf was quite what I wanted to be famous for.

"I don't think I'll tell anyone," I said. "Not yet, anyway."

Cindy watched me thoughtfully for a few more seconds. I could almost hear the clickety-clack of the little wheels and ratchets spinning around in her head.

"Good," she said finally. "Now all we have to do is figure out how you can control this thing."

I'd been afraid she was going to say something like that.

5

"Don't Shed on the Furniture"

Tuesday was practically a replay of Monday as far as waking up early and not being able to keep my mind on caddying went.

In the morning, Cindy and I went to the fairgrounds and tried to talk to the guy in the gorilla suit. We didn't really expect to find out anything, and as it turned out, we didn't. The Sevastopol Simians weren't even there. They apparently went back to Sevastopol during the day, where a couple of them had "regular jobs." All this according to a middle-aged, almost bald guy who was getting ready to open up his "knock-over-the-bottles" booth when we showed up. He hated rock music— or what the Simians called rock music, anyway— and thought stage shows in general, and this stage show in particular, had no business at fairs or carnivals. He was more than willing to answer questions about "that bunch of amateurs."

When we asked if anyone was ever "dumb enough to really believe that gorilla stunt," he just laughed. "Not with that moth-eaten ape suit he's got, they wouldn't!"

And that was that. From the fairgrounds, Cindy went somewhere to try to find that hypnotist we'd seen on the stage a couple of months ago, and I went out to the golf course. I got there a little early and talked to the guy in the pro shop, and he let me leave my bike inside with his. Three or four others were outside, chained to their regular trees, so I figured Stanley must not've tried his new racket with anyone else. Maybe he was just test-marketing it with me or something. Or maybe his little lock-picking gadget wouldn't work with the others, which I noticed were mostly combination locks. Maybe I'd get one of those, too, if I got a couple of days with good tips.

But as far as I could tell, Stanley didn't show up all that day, and by the time I was pedaling back to town along the highway, I'd almost forgotten him. Not forgiven, just forgotten, what with the other stuff on my mind.

Back in town, Cindy was waiting for me. She

had not only found out all about the hypnotist, she was all set to go see him. His stage name was "Radszyk," but his real name was Irwin Radsack, and he taught math at the high school in Bington fifteen miles away. He was taking a summer class at a university extension somewhere, but he was supposed to be back around four.

And he was, minus the fake beard and mustache he had worn onstage. Cindy and I introduced ourselves, and he looked at me and said, "Walt Cribbens? You aren't related to Wilma Cribbens, are you?"

"She's my mother. Do you know her?"

"Not exactly, but I've read all her books. And enjoyed them."

"But how did you know—"

"How did I know that 'Morgan Wilson' is really Wilma Cribbens? Very simple. I looked her up in *Contemporary Authors* last year."

"Oh." I remembered when she had gotten that questionnaire. She'd been more than willing to leave her real name out of the answers altogether, but Dad had insisted she put it in, which I guess proves that, despite what he says, he's sort of proud of what she does.

"Yes," Radsack said, "and tell her I very much enjoy her work. When I can find it, that is. I assume you know that the local bookstores, such as they are, do not even carry her books? Or anything else from her publisher?"

I knew. But Dad is just as happy that way, I think. He may be secretly proud, but he's not going to hire a brass band.

"But tell me," Radsack went on, "what can I do for you?"

The fact that he knew about Mom's books gave me an idea.

"I'd like to learn about hypnosis," I said. "I'm helping Mom do some research for her next book."

Cindy looked at me approvingly.

"Why, of course," Radsack said, smiling. "How nice, the two of you working together like that. Just what is it you wanted to know?"

"All sorts of things. But, well, for instance, can someone be hypnotized into actually changing? Physically changing, I mean?"

His eyebrows went up. "Well, it depends on what you mean by 'physically changing.' The heart rate can be increased or decreased, of course. You can raise or lower a person's blood pressure, that type of thing. Of course *I* would never attempt anything of that nature. That is for trained physicians, not hobbyists like myself."

"That's all you can do? Just change your pulse and stuff like that?"

"Oh, no, there are many changes that can be accomplished, either directly or indirectly. Tell a person a spot on his arm has been burned, and that spot will turn red as the blood rushes to it. Tell a person he's cold and he'll develop goose bumps."

"But *real* changes—you know, like in *Twilight of the Wolf*—could anything like *that* be caused by hypnosis?"

Radsack smiled. "Oh, yes, I remember that one. My favorite of your mother's books. Very realistic, despite the subject matter. But no, I don't see how anything of that nature could actually happen. Not to a human, at least. To an alien, such as the one in your mother's book, it might be another matter."

"You're sure?"

"Oh, yes, quite sure. After all, the human body is only capable of so much, and in order to change the bone and muscle structure—no, quite impossible." He stopped with a thoughtful frown.

"However," he went on, "it wouldn't be at all difficult to make someone *think* he had changed. If that is any help. I do that sort of thing all the time in my show. Have you ever seen it, by the way?"

Cindy and I both nodded. "That's why we came to talk to you," I said. "You're the only hypnotist we know of in Warrensville."

"The only *stage* hypnotist, yes," he said. "One or two of your doctors—well, they don't use it routinely, but they *have* been trained in its use. They could give you more information as to real physical changes. Perhaps I could introduce you. Doctor Sheaffer, for instance—"

"I know him," I said. "I just caddied for him yesterday."

"Well, then, you're all set."

But I wasn't, of course. Oh, I could talk to Doc Sheaffer all I wanted to any Monday, but I wasn't going to find out anything. Not anything useful, at least. This hypnosis business was a dead end, which I guess I'd known all along.

Cindy, however, was obviously not discouraged. She showed up not long after supper that evening, asking if I'd like to go to the fair again. Mom looked at me *very* suspiciously this time, and even Dad looked up from the newspaper.

"No chess tonight, son?" he asked over the top of the paper.

What with werewolfing and Stanley and everything, I'd forgotten all about Tuesday usually being chess night. I'd been thinking about trying out for the chess team at school this fall, and Dad had been giving me some practice a couple nights a week the last month or so. I was getting good enough to almost beat him with the standard bishop handicap he gave me, and he was threatening to make me start even with him one of these days, or maybe with only a pawn handicap.

But my concentration being what it was tonight, he could give me a queen and a couple of rooks and still beat me.

"I guess I don't feel like it," I said, lamely but truthfully.

He "tched" a couple of times, which only made me feel lamer, and then he went back to his paper. At least he didn't say anything about the virtues of perseverance, which I'd been more or less expecting.

But no one really objected to our going, so Cindy and I were out on the sidewalk in a couple of minutes. Then she told me what she *really* had planned for us.

"Come on," she said, tugging at my hand. "My folks took Wilbur to the fair, and they won't be back for at least a couple of hours." Wilbur is what she calls her ratty little brother. His real name is David. "We have the whole house to ourselves for a couple of hours," she went on. "And I got a book on hypnosis from the library."

I should've known better, but I went with her. It doesn't pay to argue with Cindy, even if you're a werewolf. On the way, she explained that if I wasn't able to control the way I "changed," she was fully prepared to help me along with a little hypnosis. "I read all about it before I came over. It's simple."

It didn't work, of course. At least I don't think it did. For one thing, Cindy was so impatient she stopped every minute or two to see if I was "going under" yet. Even if I had been, the interruptions would've brought me right back out.

After a half hour or so, though, just so I could say I tried, I had her quit, and I just concentrated on changing. I mean, I just sort of "saw" the change happening in my head.

I practically fainted when I actually started to change. But I didn't panic. I managed to "see" myself changing back, and sure enough, I did.

"What happened?" Cindy wanted to know. "You started getting hairy but then it all went away."

I told her.

"See!" she said triumphantly. "I told you a little hypnosis would do the trick!"

"But you didn't even hypnotize me!"

"I bet I did! You just didn't notice it, that's all!"

"How could I not notice something like that?"

"You almost didn't notice you were a *were-wolf,* Walt Cribbens! If I hadn't been along to point it out to you—"

"Okay, you win! But the important thing is, I think maybe I *can* control it, at least a little bit."

"All right," she said, "let's see you do it again. All the way this time."

"You don't have that camera up your sleeve again, do you?"

She shook her head. "I got enough evidence last night. Besides, I didn't have money for any more film. Now, are you ready to try again?"

"I guess so," I said, and started concentrating.

This time it went even faster, like I'd been doing it all my life. The whole change only took a half minute or so. Except for a single "Wow!" even Cindy was speechless.

But the big surprise to me was how I felt, and I don't mean the itching or anything like that. I mean the way I *felt!* All of a sudden I wasn't scared or worried anymore. This was *fun!*

Until right then, all I'd thought about was what had happened to all the movie werewolves

I'd seen. Mom and I—she saw a lot of late late shows, too—had always joked about how poor old Lon Chaney was always getting frozen in the ice with the Frankenstein monster or shot with a silver bullet or, the unkindest cut of all, being made to play straight for Abbott and Costello. And the others, the ones most people never heard of, like Henry Hull and John Beal and Oliver Reed, all came to pretty bad ends, too. Even the "real" werewolves in that book at the library hadn't done very well.

But *I* was different! They hadn't had any control over when they changed, but I did, and that made all the difference in the world!

I even started wondering if I could change into other things, maybe even into a real wolf. I know it may sound dumb, but the way I was feeling right then, changing into a real wolf sounded like the best idea since chocolate-covered doughnuts.

I told Cindy I was going to try.

"Now wait a minute!" she said. "A movie werewolf is one thing, but a real one— You better be careful or you'll go so far you won't be able to change back! Remember what happened to Dr. Jekyll!"

"He wasn't a werewolf, and besides, he had to

drink some kind of potion to change. Don't worry."

"Well, all right," she said with more reluctance than I'd ever heard in her voice before. She looked around the living room. "But don't shed on the furniture."

So I concentrated again. In my mind I saw myself changing, first the way I already had, and then getting more and more wolf-like, my arms turning into front legs, the whole bit.

It wasn't long, however, before I discovered there were going to be a couple of little problems that movie werewolves don't run into.

6

"I Think I'll Stick to the Movie Version"

First, there was the itching. It was *really* bad this time, and it wasn't just on my skin. It felt like it went all the way down into my bones. And I started getting dizzy. Then, with a thump, I found myself sitting on the floor, sort of.

That's when I saw what the real problem was going to be—my clothes.

My hands—which were front feet now, or paws—were sticking out of my sleeves, just barely. And my pants didn't even come close to fitting my new shape. My back feet were curled up about where my knees should have been, and my shoes were lying on the floor. One sock was inside a shoe while the other had been pulled up my pants leg. Caught on one of my claws, I suppose.

And something—a tail, I assumed—was curled up uncomfortably in the seat of my pants.

I was literally tangled up in my clothes, and I didn't dare get out of them, not with Cindy around, anyway. I mean, wolves can't dress themselves, and I didn't want to change back without getting dressed. And I was pretty sure Cindy wouldn't turn her back and wait for me, even if I threatened to bite her on the ankle.

So I changed back while I still had the chance.

I was still sitting on the floor, more or less on all fours. My clothes were still on me, but they were all twisted around. And I had to put my shoes and socks back on.

"I think I'll stick to the movie version," I said when I could talk again.

After that little episode, we went to the fair for a while. For one thing, since we'd told Mom that's where we were going, it seemed like a good idea to actually put in an appearance there so we could be seen. For another, I didn't really feel like experimenting anymore right then.

To tell the truth, I had scared myself with that last change.

I mean, being a two-legged, furry-faced, human-shaped werewolf is one thing, but a four-legged, wolf-shaped werewolf who can't even keep his clothes on was a different—and definitely weirder—situation altogether.

It didn't seem to bother Cindy all that much, however. As we walked, she tried to figure out how we could make something out of this newfound "talent" of mine. Needless to say, she didn't come up with much. Let's face it, being a werewolf, even a voluntary one, isn't the most useful thing in the world. The only idea she had that sounded the least bit practical was that we form a "hire-a-fright" company. You know, like those people you pay to hit your enemies—or your friends, I suppose, if you have a gross sense of humor—in the face with a pie. Only we would hit them in the face, so to speak, with a werewolf. I wasn't all that enthused about the idea, but Cindy made up for both of us.

To make matters worse, we hadn't been at the fair more than a few minutes when I realized the place was crawling with sheriff's deputies. We practically tripped over Sheriff Whittenberger himself. My first thought, of course, was that Stanley had gone ahead and told his uncle about Cindy and me being out late and that his uncle had believed him and now we were "under surveillance" as burglary suspects. It was a dumb idea, but you may have noticed that's practically the only kind I have unless I have a lot of time to think.

Cindy, however, had a more believable theory.

"You know why Whittenberger and everybody's here, don't you?" she asked, leaning closer and raising her voice so I could hear her over the crowd and the barkers and the rinky-dink music from the merry-go-round.

I shook my head.

"The burglaries," she said.

"How did you know—" I began, but I stopped before I could incriminate myself any further. "Why should the burglaries bring them out here?" I asked instead.

"Because Whittenberger probably thinks someone from the carnival is the burglar, that's why. People always think things like that about people just passing through a town. You know, like the gypsies in *Frankenstein Meets the Wolf Man*. Besides, the burglaries started last Saturday."

"And Saturday was the first day the fair was in town," I finished for her.

"Exactly," she said and leaned even closer. "And I'll bet someone's trying to frame them, too!"

Better them than me, I thought. "What makes you think so?" I asked.

"Come on, Walt! Anyone with the fair would have to be pretty dumb to start pulling burglaries the first night they're in town and then keep on doing it every night until they leave. You did know there were three more break-ins last night, didn't you?"

I nodded. I hadn't read the paper, but the guy in the pro shop had been talking about it when I'd brought my bicycle in. One of the club's regular golfers had been one of the victims.

"Okay, then," Cindy said and grabbed my hand. She looked around the crowded midway, spotted the "knock-over-the-bottles" booth, and started dragging me in that direction.

The same man we'd talked to the day before was in the booth, waving a handful of grungy-looking baseballs while he gave his pitch. He stopped when we came up to the little counter he stood behind. He didn't smile, but he didn't look mad, either.

Cindy, never one to waste time, launched right into her theory and had it all explained to the man in a minute or two. He made a face when she mentioned the idea that someone was setting the carnival people up for the burglaries.

"Too bad your sheriff isn't as bright as you are," he said. "Your Sheriff Whittenberger, bless his suspicious heart, is practically threatening to run us out of town."

Cindy gave me a smug, "I-told-you-so" look when the bottle-booth man turned away and started into his pitch again. Before she could gloat very much, however, we ran into the rest of her family, including Wilbur/David, who was downright ecstatic to see her. Not that he was that wild about her personally, but he knew she liked all those wild rides his folks wouldn't let him go on alone, like the Octopus and that other monster that spins you around and turns you completely upside down. And sure enough, they shelled out the ticket money for him and Cindy, and she didn't dare refuse or they would've thought she was sick or something, passing up a chance to go on all those rides, even if she did have to put up with Wilbur.

By the time that was over, Cindy's folks were ready to call it an evening, but Cindy wasn't. When she and I were alone again—except for a few hundred people milling around the midway—she explained why she had wanted to stay.

"Carmichael's here," she said. "He was on the Octopus."

I knew right away what she wanted to do. What she wanted *me* to do.

But I better explain about Carmichael. He's the assistant coach at the high school, and he teaches a couple of civics classes. He's also known as "the iceberg" and a number of other things like that. "Mr. Unflappable," for instance.

I'm not sure how it all got started, but for at least the last couple of years, it's been sort of a school tradition to try to shake him up. Nothing dangerous, you understand, just things like live snakes in his desk drawer.

But nothing ever works, absolutely nothing, and what's worse, he seems to enjoy the whole thing. Like the time someone found a real, live tarantula, a big hairy thing with a body an inch across, and put it in a cardboard box in the locker room. When Carmichael found it, he just picked up the box, looked it over a couple of seconds, took off the lid, looked another second or two, and then picked the spider up, set it on his sleeve, and gave everyone a three-minute lecture on the care and feeding of tarantulas. Then he put it back in the box, set the box down, and announced that whoever it belonged to was welcome to have it back.

So you see why I knew what Cindy wanted me to do.

"It'll be a great selling point if we ever do set

up our 'hire-a-fright' company," she said. "If it works on Mr. Carmichael, it'll work on anyone."

So, believe it or not, I agreed to try. Like I said, Cindy can be very persuasive.

We knew what his car looked like, so we went out to the parking lot and found it. I waited around there while Cindy went back inside and kept an eye on Carmichael. When he looked like he was getting ready to leave, she rushed out and told me. I scrunched down between a couple of cars a few yards away and waited. Cindy ducked down somewhere else to watch.

Carmichael showed up maybe five minutes later. A woman was with him, and since he wasn't married, I supposed it was a girl friend. Even teachers can have girl friends, I guess.

I almost stayed scrunched down and let the whole thing go by, but at the last minute I made the change to the movie-style werewolf form and jumped up and rushed toward him. The woman looked frightened enough, but Carmichael just got a grip on her arm and held her still.

When he didn't make the slightest move to run or anything else, I stumbled to a stop a couple of yards from him.

It was about then that I realized I didn't have the faintest idea what to do next.

7

"Mr. Cribbens, I Presume"

At best it was a standoff. I mean, if the way I looked didn't do the job on Carmichael, what would? I could hardly do what the werewolves do in movies, jump on him and start chewing.

Then, before I could come to my senses and run, Carmichael smiled.

"Ah," he said, "Mr. Cribbens, I presume. How nice to see you."

Worse and worse. I forgot I couldn't talk and tried to ask how he knew it was me, but all that came out were a few snarls. They bothered the girl friend but not Carmichael.

"Very good, Mr. Cribbens," he said. "If the drama department ever decides to produce *The Wolf Man,* I will be happy to recommend you for the title role. Now if you will excuse me . . . ?"

With which he dug his key out of his pocket and unlocked the passenger's side door for his girl friend. As he walked to the driver's side, he looked at me again.

"By the way, Cribbens," he said, "it's a very nice getup, but if you really want to keep your identity a secret, you shouldn't wear the same clothes you always do. Just a suggestion, mind you."

And he was in the car and starting the engine and driving away.

I changed back before anyone else could show up and make more embarrassing comments. For some reason, Cindy seemed to think the whole thing was hilarious. She didn't even seem to mind that this pretty well shot down our "hire-a-fright" idea.

"We'll think of something else," she said.

I got home around ten-thirty and got stared at a lot. After a while, Dad suggested a quick chess game, since it wasn't "really *too* late." I figured this would just make it easier for him to stare at me, but I couldn't think of a good enough reason to refuse.

I set the board up on the kitchen table, which is what we normally use. Dad came in a minute later, looked at the pieces, and raised his eyebrows almost to the front edge of his crew cut.

"As your mother knows," he said with exaggerated formality, "I am all in favor of women's lib and equality of the sexes. However, there *are* certain rules and traditions that simply cannot be discarded."

I looked more closely at the chess pieces and realized what he was getting at. I'd set them up wrong. The queen was on the king's square and vice versa.

"Sorry about that."

I made the switch and we started to play. At least Dad did. I'm not sure what I was doing. After a dozen moves, I fell into a really dumb trap and lost my queen. Then I let him pin my rook with his bishop. All I managed to do was pick a pawn now and then. And try to remember what my last move had been.

Needless to say, the game didn't last long. Dad shook his head as he stood up and looked at my lone, trapped king. "If you *do* make the chess team this fall," he said, "I hope you won't think it disloyal of me to bet on the opposition."

While I was putting the pieces back in the box, Dad headed for bed, but I noticed he stopped for a minute in the living room to talk quietly to

Mom. Then, when I was putting the board and pieces back in the bookcase in the hall, Mom came to the living room door. She watched me while I fumbled with the box, which just made me that much more twitchy.

"Is something bothering you, Walt?" she asked finally.

"What could be bothering me?" Not a very original line, but it was all that came to me.

"I don't know," she said, "but you seem a little on edge. Something happen at the fair?"

I shook my head, hoping that Carmichael wasn't going to tell too many people about "that silly Cribbens kid and his wolf mask."

"Half the sheriff's department was there," I said. "Guess they think someone at the fair is doing the burglaries. Must've made me nervous."

She kept on looking at me. "You're sure that's all?"

I shrugged. "Except that school starts again in a couple of weeks." The start of school could be used to explain almost anything.

She didn't say anything for what seemed like about five and a half hours, and all I could do was try to keep from fidgeting too much. She looked like she was going to say something a couple of times, but she didn't. For a few panicky seconds, while I remembered how she'd asked me if something had happened at the fair, I wondered again if she might actually be thinking I was mixed up with the burglaries and was just using going to the fair as an excuse to get out of the house. Of course I *was* using the fair as an excuse to get out of the house, but not so I could do burglaries, but I could hardly tell her that.

"All right," she said finally. "But just remember, if there's anything bothering you, or if anything happens that you don't understand—anything at all—you can talk to me about it. Okay?"

"Okay."

What else was I going to say? *Hey, Mom, I just found out I'm a werewolf, but there's nothing to worry about. I've got it under control.*

Sure. Mom's understanding and open-minded and all those good things, but there are limits.

I went to bed early, but again I couldn't get to sleep. And as I lay there, everything that had happened during the evening kept kicking around in my head. The strange thing was, the more it all bounced around, the more I kept going back to the first time that I realized I really could change at will. All the other stuff—the shock when the change to a real wolf hadn't worked out quite the way it should have, the fiasco with Carmichael—sort of faded away.

And the more I remembered about that first voluntary change, the more I realized how good, how really *good* it had felt. Sure, it itched like crazy for a few seconds, and the whole thing scared me silly for a while, but to think that I could change whenever I wanted to . . . !

In a weird sort of way, it was kind of like your first date. You're sweating and nervous and it doesn't turn out anything like you expected and you make all kinds of really dumb mistakes, but all you remember is the good-night kiss on the porch and you can't wait for the next one. Which should give you some idea of how wacked out I was, comparing turning into a werewolf to a date.

Anyway, about one o'clock I got out of bed. The last sound I'd heard from Mom or Dad had been almost an hour ago.

I went to the window and looked out. We lived in a single-floor ranch-style house, so the window was only four or five feet off the ground. It looked out over the backyard, which had shrubs around it, not a fence. I couldn't see lights in any of the nearby houses.

I opened the window, raised the screen, and

stuck my head out. My heart was beating like crazy and I was tingly all over. I was thinking what fun it would be to change all the way to the four-legged version and just be out there running around. Skinny-dipping in a wolf suit, so to speak.

And I started wondering just how long this werewolf thing had been sneaking up on me. I mean, werewolves are night people, right? Not as much as vampires, maybe, but definitely night people. And the last three or four years, I'd been really hating to go to bed early or get up early. And that night last year, when I'd been coming back from Uncle Jerry's place in Indianapolis and I missed the early evening bus and didn't get back to Warrensville until almost three in the morning —I got a real charge out of that, more than from the visit to Uncle Jerry's, that's for sure. I hadn't been the least bit sleepy, and I watched out the bus window the whole trip.

"Just a stage you're going through," Dad always said, "like your mother when she was your age. Why, when I first met her, she insisted she couldn't possibly go to sleep before midnight. Sheer nonsense, of course. She outgrew it, and I'm sure you will, too."

I had halfway believed him—until now.

Slowly, I changed, first to the movie version, then to the real thing. I should've gotten out of my pajamas first, I realized, but I managed anyway. I probably left a couple claw and tooth marks in them, but I made it.

I leaped out the window. And instantly panicked.

Could I get back in?

I leaped up to the window and scrabbled inside. My claws on the windowsill made a racket you wouldn't believe, and I was sure the whole block, if not the whole town, would wake up.

But there wasn't a sound once I got inside on the rug. I sat crouched by my pajamas, ready to change back and get dressed fast if I heard anyone in the hall or a siren or anything, but nothing happened. Nobody woke up.

Okay, I thought, *I can get back in.*

I listened another minute or two and then leaped back out the window.

But now that I was out here, what was I going to do? I'd been thinking how much fun it would be to just run around, but how much running could I do in our backyard?

I looked around, wondering if I dared leave

the yard in this form, and that's when I got the biggest scare of my werewolf career up to that point. There, not three feet away, looking right at me, was the awfullest-looking thing I'd ever seen.

8

"Besides, He'd Probably Taste Terrible"

This thing, whatever it was, looked vaguely like the biggest, hairiest dog you can imagine, but the head—well, the head was *really* big, twice as big as any dog's head had a right to be. And a flat nose, like a giant bulldog's. It was about as ugly as you can imagine, with stiff, bristly hair all over it.

It was, of course, me.

My reflection, in one of our basement windows.

Once I figured that out, I was all right. More or less. My respect for Cindy went up another notch when I realized that she had stayed cool when this identical thing had appeared in the same room with her, and I wondered if maybe she was related to Carmichael. The movie version of me was absolutely gorgeous compared to this.

That's when I started thinking about Cindy's "hire-a-fright" idea again. In *this* form it might really work.

For a second I thought of trying Carmichael again, but only for a second. Maybe someday, after I'd gotten a lot of practice, but not now. Once was enough.

But then I thought of Stanley. Stanley Olinger and his junior-league protection racket.

Now *there* was someone who really deserved a good jolt, if not an actual bite or two. Him and his two buddies, Willard Tucker and Tim Stratton.

I looked at my reflection in the basement window again. I tried an experimental snarl. Beautiful! If this didn't turn Stanley into a quivering heap, nothing would.

And he lived only three or four blocks away.

I was halfway there, skulking along through the alleys, when I realized I had the same kind of problem I'd already run into with Carmichael. That is, I didn't have much of an idea what I was actually going to do. Scratch on his bedroom window and snarl? Well, it was better than nothing, I suppose. Maybe next time I could bring a note in my teeth. "I've got my eye on you, Stanley! Behave yourself or you're really going to get it! Signed, the Werewolf of Warrensville."

It had a nice ring to it, I thought. Or maybe in my wolf shape I just didn't have good sense, I don't know.

But I'd think of *something*. Maybe chew the screen out of his window and get inside and jump up on his bed and be standing over him when he woke up.

But the problem never came up because Stanley wasn't home. His car, that '57 Plymouth he'd gotten for his sixteenth birthday, wasn't in the driveway or anywhere at the curb.

I looked around a little, but I took off when some little, woolly dog next door started yapping its head off. I suppose it could smell me, and I probably smelled funny. A half-dozen dogs of all sizes had acted the same way on the way over. None of them had actually attacked, but they'd done a lot of barking and howling, all from a safe distance or from behind a fence. The only thing that got up the nerve to take a run at me was a cat, a small gray one with more hair than sense, and that made me wonder if my being a werewolf had anything to do with the fact that most cats didn't seem to like me. I mean, I like cats and all that, and if I really work at it, I can get one to sit still and put up with being petted, but usually not for long. Which is just as well, I suppose, since Mom is allergic to them.

I was starting for home when I thought about Stanley's two buddies again, Willard and Tim. Tim Stratton lived only a couple of blocks over, so I might as well go past and take a look.

It was a small, two-story house on a narrow lot, and at first I didn't think anyone was home there, either, but then I went around the side of the house to the garage in back.

And there in the alley just outside the open garage door were Stanley and his car. And Willard and Tim!

Jackpot!

I didn't really think beyond the next ten seconds, maybe not even that far. I guess it was just my natural werewolfish high spirits or something, but whatever it was, I ran full tilt around the side of the garage and into the alley, snarling my huge and disgusting-looking head off.

There was instant chaos, kind of like when a dog runs into a crowded chicken coop. Stanley dropped something he'd been taking out of the trunk of his car. Almost before it hit the concrete with a loud popping noise, all three of them were scrambling in different directions. Stanley made it inside his car in Olympic time, but not before my teeth made a nice large rip in the cuff of his still neatly pressed slacks. Willard ran around the garage into the yard, and Tim shot inside the garage itself and tried frantically to pull down the overhead door but only succeeded in tearing the pull cord loose. And a dog across the alley started barking.

I could've gotten either of them without half trying, but I held back. I was mainly interested in Stanley, and I *probably* could've gotten his leg instead of just the cuff, but I was just as glad I hadn't. For one thing, for all I knew, a bite might turn *him* into a werewolf, and he's enough trouble just being a human.

Besides, I thought, *he'd probably taste terrible.*

So I just stood there on all fours, snarling while Willard vanished altogether and Tim finally got the garage door down. I turned around and gave Stanley, who was crouched wide-eyed in his car, a final snarl that made him duck back from the window.

About then, a light came on in the house across the alley, probably the one that belonged to the barking dog. I gave Stanley one last snarl and ran. I almost fell over the thing he'd dropped behind the car a few seconds before—a small TV set

with, now that it'd been dropped, a broken picture tube—but then I was through another yard and out of sight.

I ran all the way home. Wolves can't laugh, I guess, or I would've been laughing all the way home, too. *That* had been *fun!* Dumb and pointless, maybe, but *fun!* And that rip in Stanley's slacks would cost at *least* as much to fix as he'd gotten from me at the golf course.

It wasn't until the next morning that I found out there was a serious side to the affair.

A very serious side.

9

"I'm Just a Werewolf, Not Spiderman"

I was still arguing with myself when I got to Cindy's door the next morning, another bright, sunny day. Should I tell her about last night or not? I probably would, I thought as I rang the bell. For one thing, I had to let *someone* know about the panicked look on Stanley's face or I'd explode. The trouble was, she'd just decide that her "hire-a-fright" idea was a good one after all.

When Cindy opened the door, she looked surprised to see me.

"Oh. It's you. Hi."

But before I could say anything, her mother was there. "Who—" she began, but then she saw me. "Oh, it's you." *That expression must run in the family today,* I thought.

"Something wrong?" I asked.

"We were robbed last night," Cindy said. "Somebody broke in a window and swiped a bunch of stuff."

"Yes," her mother said, "and we were expecting someone any minute to repair the window. We thought that's who you were."

I wasn't sure what to say. I felt a little odd. It's one thing to hear about other people having their houses broken into, but when it happens this close to home, it's something else.

"I'm sorry," was all I could come up with.

"That's all right," Mrs. Deardorf said. Then she grinned weakly and shrugged. "They didn't get much, really, and David is thrilled. He's out telling all his friends about the big robbery."

The ratty little brother. He's the type that would do that, too.

"What did they get?" I asked.

"The biggest item was the stereo," she said, "but it was almost ten years old. A little jewelry, nothing expensive, and some money Mr. Deardorf left on our bureau." She laughed and shook her head. "He didn't want to carry too much cash in his wallet when we went to the fair. He was afraid someone might pick his pocket."

"And they got my TV set, don't forget," Cindy said.

"Yes, Cindy's little portable. I suppose the console in the living room was too big for them. Or they were in too much of a hurry." Mrs. Deardorf leaned forward confidentially. "I think they were still here when we drove up," she said. "I heard a car in the alley just after we came in, and the back door was still open."

I didn't pay much attention to her last two or three sentences, I'm afraid. I was thinking about "Cindy's little portable," and for the next five minutes, while I waited for Cindy to get ready to follow me outside, I nearly went buggy. But finally we were out on the sidewalk.

"I saw your TV set last night and I know who the burglars are," I burst out.

For once in her life, Cindy seemed at a loss for words, which gave me a chance to rush through the story of my little field trip the night before.

"And that thing that Stanley dropped," I finished, "I'd swear it was your little TV set."

"So *that's* what he was doing in that alley Sunday night!" she exclaimed, snapping her fingers. "I bet they'd just finished doing a job!"

"Probably," I said. This also explained Stanley's dumb remark to me the next afternoon at the golf course. A good offense is the best defense, so he'd threatened to tell his uncle about *me* before I could threaten to tell anyone about *him*. And he'd made a couple of bucks with my bike at the same time.

"Come on," Cindy said. "Let's tell Mom. She can call the sheriff."

"Now wait a minute!" I grabbed her arm to keep her from dashing back in the house. "What are you going to tell her? That I was out werewolfing last night and I just happened to see the burglars?"

"We don't have to tell her about the werewolfing part, just that—"

"Just that I was out for a stroll? At two in the morning? Come on! You know how slick Stanley is. If they arrest *anyone*, it'll be *me!* And even if they don't, my folks will want to know what I was doing out at that time of night! They're already looking at me kind of funny, and you *know* how good I am at keeping secrets!"

"But we've got to do *something!* We can't just let them get away with it! How about an anonymous phone call? I'll bet those guys were just storing the stuff they got last night in Tim's garage. Everything is probably there right now."

"You really think Whittenberger or anyone

down there is going to pay any attention to some kid who won't even give his name?"

"They'll at least check it out. Won't they?"

"I don't know. Maybe, if we're lucky."

"All right, it's settled. Unless you can think of something better."

I couldn't, so for the next few minutes I practiced making my voice deeper, which was pretty much of a lost cause right from the start. I'd be lucky if I didn't break out in a squeak. Then we fussed for a good half hour over what I should say. Cindy wanted something "with a little imagination," but I held out for "simple and short." Since I was the one who would have to deliver it, Cindy finally gave in. She even made a cue card for me to read it from:

"If you want to find some of the things taken in the burglaries this week, look in the Stratton garage," and then the address.

It took another half hour to find a phone where I wouldn't be seen or overheard and another ten minutes to work up the nerve to actually use it. The phone was in the basement of the courthouse, and Cindy kept watch up and down the long, echoing corridor while I stumbled through the call.

The instant I hung up and took the wadded-up handkerchief out of the mouthpiece, we ran. I was pretty sure calls couldn't be traced that fast, but I didn't want to be anywhere near *any* phone for a while.

Cindy wanted to stake out the Stratton garage and watch for Whittenberger or some deputy to show up, but I talked her out of it. "It'd look suspicious if we were right there, applauding."

I didn't have any caddying jobs lined up that afternoon, but after a quick lunch under Mom's increasingly suspicious eye, I went out to the course anyway. Some days I was able to pick up an unscheduled job, and, luckily, this was one of those days. It kept me busy and got me through the afternoon without a nervous breakdown, though I'm not so sure about the poor guy I caddied for. I probably did an even worse job than I'd been doing the last two days.

On the way over to Cindy's on my bicycle afterward, I practically got zapped when I didn't slow down enough for a stop sign, and to make matters worse, apparently our call to Whittenberger hadn't had any results at all. No one had called the Deardorfs to let them know their stolen property had been recovered or anything else.

It wasn't until the afternoon paper came out that we found out what had happened. A little item on the back page explained it all.

"Prank Call," the small headline said. The article underneath told how "an unidentified juvenile" had called the sheriff's office. The caller was "obviously attempting to disguise his or her voice" and spoke of objects stolen in the "recent wave of burglaries," saying they could be found in a certain garage. The owner of the garage was not identified because "the allegations were checked and nothing was found." The theory, advanced by Sheriff Whittenberger, was that the caller was either a misguided practical joker or someone who "bore a grudge against the owner of the garage in question."

"You're *sure* about that TV set you saw?" Cindy asked when we finished reading the article.

"I'm sure."

"Then what happened? Where is everything?"

"How should I know?"

"I told you we should've staked the place out!"

"Look, it could be anywhere. Maybe after what happened last night, they decided to move the stuff somewhere else. I mean, there was a lot of noise and carrying-on. I think a couple of the neighbors were coming out to see what was going on. Or maybe they weren't moving stuff into the garage at all. Maybe Stanley was just giving Tim your set for himself."

"So what do we do now?"

"Who said we were going to do *anything?*"

"You're going to let them get away with it?" She made a face like she couldn't believe what she was hearing.

"Look," I said, "I'm just a werewolf, not Spiderman! What *can* I do?"

"You could follow them around and find out where the stuff is really hidden."

"And how do I do that, for crying out loud? They have a car, remember?"

"In your wolf form—"

"Sure! That's easy for you to say! You know what happens to dogs that chase cars, don't you?"

"You've got more brains than a dog, Walt Cribbens! At least I always thought you did."

"I've got brains enough to know this idea of yours won't work! In the first place, I'm nowhere near as fast as a car—or a speeding bullet, for that matter. In the second, I can't pass for a decent *wolf,* let alone a dog. Didn't you get a good look at me yesterday evening? If anybody sees *that* thing galloping down the street after cars or anything else, they'll start looking for the flying saucer it came out of. Half the county, including the sheriff, will be out gunning for me."

When I stopped, she just looked at me a couple of seconds. "Are you through?"

I nodded.

"Okay," she said. "Just don't worry. I'll think of something."

"That's what I'm afraid of," I said, and went home for supper. Despite what common sense told me, I had the feeling that this was going to be a hairy sort of an evening, in more ways than one.

10

"I Don't Suppose You Werewolves Can Pick Locks"

Cindy did, of course, think of something. Unfortunately, it wasn't up to her usual standards. All it really amounted to was breaking and entering with a camera, the same instant job she had used to take the pictures of me while I was changing.

She had the camera with her when she came over a few minutes after supper, and she was wearing the darkest clothes she had been able to find. All she needed was some dirt smudged on her face and she'd look like a commando raiding party's mascot.

"It's simple," she explained after she yanked me out on the porch so we could talk without my folks hearing. "All that stuff they've stolen has to be *somewhere*. The paper said they'd gotten a half-dozen TV sets and stereos and at least two video recorders, and that stuff isn't small. It's too much to keep in the trunk of a car. Now we know it isn't in Tim's garage, and Stanley's folks don't even have a garage, so there's no place it *can* be except Willard's."

"What makes you think it's in a garage at all?"

"Where else? A hollow tree in the park?"

"What about inside one of their houses?"

She shook her head and gave me a "how-could-you-be-so-dumb" look. "Where their folks could stumble over it? Could you hide that much stuff in *your* house? No, if that garage is anything like ours, that's where everything is. In ours, there's a platform, a sort of storage area, up over the cars. Nobody's looked up there for years."

"But you don't know if Willard's garage has anything like that. Do you?"

She shrugged. "We'll never know if we don't look. Besides, can you think of anything better?"

"Yes. How about forgetting the whole thing?"

"How about me showing those pictures of you to your folks?"

So we went. Not that it was totally because of her threat. In fact, I was probably just looking for an excuse to go ahead, and that was as good as any.

We told everyone we were going to the fair—again. From the way both Mom and Dad looked at me—or the way I thought they looked at me—I was sure they figured Cindy and I were the burglars, and I wouldn't blame them if they did.

Willard Tucker lived on the other side of town, more than a mile away, so it took twenty or thirty minutes to walk there. The timing worked out about right, though. It was getting dark, and, since most of the burglaries took place not long after dark, when the victims were at the fair like Cindy's folks had been, chances were pretty good that Willard would be out burgling with Stanley.

There weren't any lights on in the house when we got there. Willard's folks—he was an only child, like me—were probably out, too, maybe even at the fair.

Cautiously, we sneaked into the alley and tried the large overhead door.

It was locked.

"I don't suppose you werewolves are any good at picking locks?" Cindy said.

I shook my head. "Unless you want me to try to bite the lock off."

She hmphed at me and said, "There must be another door."

There was. It was on the back side of the garage, facing the house, and it wasn't even latched, let alone locked.

It was no wonder it wasn't locked, we decided, after looking around inside for a minute or two. There was nothing in there but some oil spots on the floor, a rake with some missing teeth, and a lawn mower that was older than Cindy and me put together. No storage area, nothing.

However, in the yard right next to the garage was one of those little sheds, the kind that looks like a miniature barn six or seven feet square.

And the shed was solidly padlocked.

Cindy was wondering where the nearest screw-driver was so we could try to unscrew the hinges, but before we had a chance to do anything, a car stopped in the alley right behind the garage and we heard someone getting out.

Cindy and I both ran for the house and ducked around the corner.

I almost bolted when we looked back around the corner and saw Stanley and his two buddies, Tim Stratton and Willard Tucker, coming around the garage. They looked a lot tougher to me now than they had last night.

But then I noticed that Willard didn't look nearly as menacing as the other two. In fact, he looked like he'd much sooner be somewhere else altogether. Stanley had to give him a shove every other step or two to keep him moving.

"Come on, Stan," Willard said, "cut it out!"

"I'll cut it out when this thing is over. Now keep moving." Stanley was using his movie-tough-guy voice now, not the butter-wouldn't-melt-in-his-mouth voice he uses with his teachers all the time. Like I said before, whatever else you can say about Stanley, he's adaptable.

Stanley gave Willard another nudge, and they all three stopped in front of the miniature barn.

"Open it," Stanley said.

Willard obeyed, but he didn't look or sound happy about it. "I don't like this," he said in a protesting whisper.

"Then let's get it over with in a hurry," Stanley said, "before your folks get back. Or before someone makes an anonymous call about *your* garage."

"All right, all right!" Willard said. He still sounded unhappy, but he found a key and opened the padlock. When the door was open, he stood back and waved Stanley inside. "This is your idea, so you pick something out."

"Of course," Stanley said and ducked inside.

We heard him moving things around, and pretty soon he came back out. He held a big, clunky necklace in one hand. I couldn't see it very

well in the poor light, but I felt Cindy twitch where she was crouched in front of me, and I was ready to bet that she recognized the necklace. It was probably one of her mother's, swiped in the burglary last night.

"Just the thing," Stanley was saying. "It's not worth much, so we won't lose a lot of money. And it's easy to recognize, and it'll be easy to smuggle into the fairgrounds and ditch in someone's trailer."

So they *were* planning to frame someone at the fair, which wasn't all that much of a surprise. I mean, the way they started their little crime wave the same day the fair came to town, they must've had something like this in mind all the time. Whittenberger's looking through Tim's garage probably just speeded things up a little.

I nudged Cindy and made some spastic motions indicating we should get out of there.

When we were safely out of earshot a block away, we stopped.

"We *have* to call the sheriff *now!*" Cindy said.

"What makes you think they'll pay any attention? After the false alarm this morning, we'll be lucky if they don't hang up without even listening."

"So what else *can* we do?"

"*I* don't know. You're the one who— Look,

you go ahead and call, but make up some kind of story. Say you just overheard them talking or something. You know, bragging about all the stuff they had in Willard's shed. And—and tell them you're afraid to tell them your name."

"And what are *you* going to be doing while I'm doing all this?"

"It's only a mile or so to the fairgrounds. I'll run over there and see if I can keep track of Stanley and that necklace. Or warn someone, like that guy we talked to at the bottle booth."

So I left Cindy to find herself a pay phone and I ran. After a couple of blocks, I started panting and wished I had my bicycle even if it didn't have a light and Mom would ground me for a month if I took it out after dark. On one deserted stretch by the railroad tracks, I even tried changing to the movie-version werewolf, but it only made things worse. Not only was I still panting, but my tongue started hanging out and my shoes didn't fit and my feet hurt.

I got to the fairgrounds in eight or ten minutes, but it took me another five to catch my breath.

I was in luck, though. I was almost through panting and sweating when Stanley and his two friends showed up in the parking lot in Stanley's car. They must've done some more planning before they came over. I just hoped their plans didn't include keeping a close lookout for anyone tailing them.

Apparently they weren't worrying about being followed. Once they got inside the midway, they didn't look around at all. They just wandered through the noisy crowd doing their best to look innocent. Stanley was good at it but the others just looked nervous, particularly Willard.

But then they split up, and I was stuck. After a few seconds though, I decided to stick with Stanley. He was the one who had had the necklace last, and he probably wouldn't trust anyone else with it. He certainly wouldn't trust anyone else to do the actual planting.

In a couple of minutes, I saw that I was right. Stanley wandered down toward the end of the row of midway tents and suddenly ducked around to the back, which was where the carnival people's cars and trucks and trailers and things were parked.

I peeked around the corner of the tent. Most of the trailers and vans were backed up against a high, chain link fence, but the trucks that carried the disassembled midway rides were scattered over the whole area.

Stanley was disappearing around one of the flatbed trucks. He still had another three or four to go around before he would be at the line of trailers and vans.

Keeping low and feeling like I was acting in a bad movie, I followed.

In a few seconds I was at the truck Stanley had gone around. I poked my head cautiously around a huge rear tire.

Stanley was nowhere in sight, so I figured he had just kept on going. I put on a little more speed and pretty soon I was looking out around the last of the trucks, right toward the line of trailers and vans.

I still couldn't see Stanley. That was when I started worrying.

If I'd had good sense, of course, I would've turned around and run back to the midway as fast as I could. But if I'd had good sense, I wouldn't've been back here in the first place.

I was trying to figure out what to do when I heard something behind me, and I realized what must have happened. Stanley had heard me behind him, and he had doubled back, around the trucks.

And now *he* was behind *me*.

Without really thinking—why should I change and start now?—I ran for the trailers and vans. A second later, I was ducking between a big, plain trailer and a bright yellow van with "Sevastopol Simians" painted in orange lightning-bolt letters on the side. I guess I was hoping there would be room enough between the backs of the various vehicles and the fence for me to squeeze through.

But there wasn't.

And by the time I decided I should try to climb the fence, it was too late. I could hear Stanley only a few yards from the little aisle I was in, and he was heading straight for me.

11

"That Is the Ugliest *Dog* *I've Ever Seen"*

The next thing I knew, Stanley had stopped a few feet from the end of the van.

"All right," he said in his toughest voice, "whoever you are in there, you've had it!"

I felt just the teensiest bit of relief then, when his "whoever you are" made me realize he at least didn't know who I was. Yet.

So I did the only thing I could think of to do. I changed to the movie version. I figured that if I charged out at him looking like that, hairy face and fangs and furry paws, he'd be too startled to grab me—or to recognize my clothes the way Carmichael had. He might even run himself. I'd worry later about changing back without anyone seeing me. If the Hulk can get away with it, why couldn't I?

I'd just finished changing and was bracing myself to make a run at Stanley when a new voice practically made me jump right out of my hairy skin.

"Wow!" it said, practically in my ear. "That is a truly *fantastic* wolf trick!"

"Yeah," said another voice not much farther away, "but you didn't have to sneak in here like this to audition it for us. If you can do anything in the band, anything at all, even keep time by pounding the cymbals, you've got a job whenever you want it!"

I saw them then. Two of the Sevastopol Simians, their shiny, metallic outfits looking a little ratty at such close range, were in the half-open door to their van. They must've been resting up for their next show and heard Stanley yelling at me and then opened their van door while I wasn't looking.

And they must have seen me while I changed into this hairy creature.

They'd seen me!

I was so shook up, I almost changed the rest of the way, into the four-legged variety, but I only went a little ways before I got control again, at least of my shape.

My legs were another matter. They ran, without a whole lot of advice from my head.

Stanley, who had appeared around the corner of the trailer, let out a most un-Stanleyish squeak and jumped backward. He tripped over something, probably his own feet, and just stared up as I leaped over him.

I kept on running, darting through the mass of trucks. My feet hurt like crazy because my shoes didn't fit my werewolfish feet, but I didn't stop. Behind me I could hear the two Simians yelling for me to come back, but at least they weren't chasing me.

And neither was Stanley.

Between the trucks and the end of the midway tents, no one was in sight and I had the presence of mind to pause long enough to turn human again. It went really fast this time, maybe because I was getting better each time, or maybe because of sheer panic.

Without looking back, I rushed out into the crowd on the midway. I got a couple of odd looks from people I bumped into, but there was no one I recognized.

When my mind started working again, I looked around for the bottle booth. The guy that ran it might not be a really close friend, but at least he knew who I was. And Cindy and I had already talked to him about the burglaries. I should've gone to him before, instead of waiting for Stanley to show up.

When I got to the bottle booth, the man was doing good business, but he leaned over the counter toward me when I waved to him nervously.

"More trouble, kid?"

"Probably," I said. "One of the burglars is back there around your trailers right now. He's trying to frame you people by dumping a stolen necklace in a trailer."

The man stood up straight, frowning. "How do you—" he started, but then he stopped. I guess he figured it didn't matter how I knew, at least not right then.

"Sorry, folks," he said loudly to the waiting customers, "but we're closing for a few minutes."

He stuffed the baseballs in the huge pockets of his apron and scrambled over the counter and headed for the next booth, where a couple of people were throwing darts at balloons. The bottle man spoke briefly to the operator of the dart booth, and the two of them took off together. The dart man took a handful of darts with him.

They disappeared around the end of the tents,

and I just stood there, waiting. The first smart thing I'd done all day.

Three or four minutes later, Cindy showed up. She was a little out of breath, but not as bad as I had been. Either she was in better condition or she hadn't run the whole mile the way I did.

"They wouldn't listen," she said before I had a chance to ask her anything. "I guess I shouldn't have told them Stanley was involved. Anyway, Whittenberger blew up and wouldn't listen to a thing I said. His nephew can't do anything wrong, I guess. Now what's happening around here? Any luck with Stanley?"

I told her what had happened. By the time I'd finished, the two men were back, shaking their heads.

"Thanks, kid," the bottle-booth man said, "but whoever it was got away. Those guys in the Simians *said* they saw someone climb the fence into the parking lot."

"Yeah, but they also said they saw a guy change into a wolf," the dart man said, "which means they're probably just imagining things." He sighed. "Assuming there really was a burglar back there, I don't suppose you have any idea who it was?"

"As a matter of fact, we do," Cindy said.

The dart man blinked, seeing Cindy for the first time. "Who's this?"

The bottle-booth man explained, more or less, and then Cindy and I told them pretty much the same story she had told the sheriff on the phone. That is, that we'd heard Stanley and the others talking about the loot and how they were going to frame someone here at the fair and how I'd followed them. We even told them where the loot was hidden.

"Maybe the sheriff will pay attention to *you,*" Cindy said. "They sure won't listen to me."

"They *better* listen to us!" the bottle-booth man said, and he and the dart man stalked away, looking for a deputy.

I was starting to relax, figuring we'd done everything we could, but then Cindy changed my mind.

"You know what's going to happen, don't you?" she said. "By the time anyone gets over to Willard's place, they'll have everything moved again! That shed will be empty!"

"We better warn those two, then," I said, but when I looked around, the two men were nowhere to be seen.

"I'll look for them," Cindy said. "You go try to keep Stanley from moving that stuff out of the shed."

Forty-eight hours ago, or even twenty-four, I would've said "Forget it!" But now— Well, I didn't even take time to think about it. Maybe I *was* beginning to think I was Spiderman instead of just a werewolf.

Anyway, I took off running again while Cindy started searching through the crowd for the bottle-booth man and his friend. What I hoped, I guess, or maybe even expected, was that Willard's folks would be home by now and all I'd have to do would be pound on the door and get them out in the backyard and tell them what was in the shed.

But no such luck, of course. The house was still dark when I stumbled to a stop in front of it. I was totally out of breath again, and there was no sign of any sheriff's department cars.

When I got my breathing under control, I eased along the side of the house and peeked around the same corner Cindy and I had been looking around before.

Sure enough, there they were, all three of them. Two cars were in the alley, and Willard was opening the shed. As I watched, Stanley pushed past Willard. Stanley looked a little mussed, probably from when he tripped backing away from me or when he climbed the fence to the fair parking lot. There was a little noise inside the shed, and then Stanley was stalking out with a large portable TV set in his hands.

They'll have it all carted away in five or ten minutes, I thought, long before anyone else can get here.

So I changed—all the way.

The movie version wouldn't work, not with all three of them. Once they got a good look at me in that form, they'd probably start thinking the same way Carmichael had—just some dumb kid in a Halloween getup. And that would be that.

But the four-legged variety was something else. I hoped. It had worked once, so maybe it would work again.

Somehow, I managed to wiggle and claw my way out of the clothes that were tangled all over my now-four-footed body. I even took an extra few seconds to use my paws and nose to pile them up in as much of a bundle as I could. I figured that, if I had to, I could grab most of them—or at least my trousers, with my identification in the pockets—in my teeth and take off with them.

By the time I had my clothes piled up and more or less pushed out of sight under a bush, I was wondering if Clark Kent had this much trouble in those phone booths. At least Spiderman was able to wrap everything up in webbing and stick it to a wall somewhere.

Unfortunately, Stanley and his buddies had made two or three trips by then. They probably had the shed half empty already.

Pulling in a deep breath—which sounded vaguely like a small howl, I noticed—I charged around the corner of the house, snarling and showing as many fangy teeth as I could.

Their first reaction was about what it had been the night before. They scattered.

Willard jumped inside the shed and pulled the doors shut after him. Tim and Stanley scrambled through the unlocked garage door and slammed it. I could see their faces looking out through the small glass panes at the top.

Okay, I thought as I kept on snarling, *what do I do now? Sooner or later they're going to realize I'm all bark and no bite.*

Bark? Well, maybe that was the answer. It would be best if the sheriff showed up, but I'd settle for anyone at this point. A neighbor complaining about a noisy dog, a passing pedestrian, anyone.

I tried barking, but it didn't work. I guess

werewolves don't bark. I tried a couple of howls, but they weren't a lot better. Not really loud, and what I needed was volume.

And while I was doing all this worrying and experimenting with my PA system, the two in the garage were starting to look more puzzled and less afraid. I gave them a couple more snarls and lunged at the door again.

But it didn't hold them very long. In another minute or two, they started edging the door open. And Stanley, I could see through the crack, had taken his belt off. It was one of those heavy things with a buckle like a paperweight. He had the belt wrapped around his fist with the buckle swinging free, like a mace.

I lunged again, and he flinched and slammed the door shut, but I knew it wouldn't work many more times.

And if he got out where he could swing that buckle, I'd be in real trouble.

I turned and ran to the front of the house, hoping to see someone walking by or looking out a window or something. And I was in luck, sort of. A car was just pulling up across the street. There were two couples in it, and I recognized one of the boys as a senior at high school.

How was it Lassie did it? I wondered.

Trying to look as appealing as I could—which wasn't very appealing, considering what this head and bristle-brush face looked like—I ran up to the car. I sat quietly except for some heavy breathing, which came out, luckily, like a sort of doggy whimper.

One of the boys got out, and his eyes widened when he saw me.

"Hey, look at this," he said to the others, and in a few seconds they were all coming toward me cautiously.

"What kind is it?" one of the girls asked.

"I've never seen one like *this!*" the other said.

"A mutated bulldog or something?" one of the boys said.

"Whatever it is," the one I'd recognized said, "that is the *ugliest* dog I've ever seen."

Then he reached down to pet me. As carefully as I could, I grabbed his jacket sleeve in my teeth.

He jerked back but I held on.

"Come on, dog! Let go! That's my good jacket!"

I tried motioning with my head toward the backyard of the Tucker place across the street. I even made more doggy noises.

"I think he's trying to tell us something," one

of the girls said. "Aren't you, boy?" She patted me on the head.

"He's slobbering all over my good jacket is what he's doing!" the one I was holding said. Then, with a jerk that hurt my teeth, he pulled loose. "Let's get out of here," he said.

And that was that. They headed for the house they had parked in front of, and no matter how much twitching and whining I did, they ignored me. Trying to grab the pants leg of one boy just got me a whack on the side of the head.

Desperate, I dashed back to the Tucker yard. All three burglars were loading again. Another lunge and a snarl or three got them back in the garage.

But this time it lasted only a minute. Then the others started opening the door slowly while Stanley swung that head-breaking belt buckle.

This was it, I thought. They were going to get away with it.

But then I thought, *So what? Why am I so worked up? Is it worth a broken head? Who said werewolves are supposed to be heroes anyway?*

I backed away, but I was still thinking. Maybe I could chew a hole in their tires, except they'd probably turn out to be steel-belted radials.

But now all three were coming out of the garage. The other two had their belts off, too. The buckles weren't as big as Stanley's, but they'd hurt if they caught me.

And that's when Whittenberger and two of his deputies showed up. Two came around the garage from the alley and one from along the side of the house.

I breathed a sigh of relief and stopped snarling.

But the relief lasted only a few seconds. The deputies were watching the burglars, but Whittenberger was watching me.

And he had his gun pointed right at me.

12

"Even Werewolves Need an Education"

"That dog's crazy!" Stanley said loudly. "It was trying to kill us!"

"Yeah!" Willard yelled. "It was foaming at the mouth!"

I guess they were trying for any kind of distraction they could find. If they could get the deputies to chase me, they might have another minute or two to get the last load in the cars before anyone actually looked in the shed.

Anyway, I was a pretty good distraction, from the looks of it. I wasn't a mad dog, but I had been acting pretty much like one. And I probably looked a lot worse than I was acting.

Whittenberger, of course, seemed to be taking his nephew at his word, though the deputies looked dubious.

I started to move forward, don't ask me why. Maybe to try to explain, as if I had vocal cords and all that stuff in this shape.

My moving only made it worse. I saw Whittenberger's finger tightening on the trigger.

Great. I'd kept the burglars here, and the sheriff was going to shoot *me* if I wasn't careful. Probably even if I *was* careful. If he thought I had rabies, it was the only sensible thing for him to do.

But even if he didn't shoot me, I was in trouble. At the very least, I'd end up in the pound, and then what could I do? If a vet saw me, he'd know I wasn't a real dog. And even if he didn't notice anything, I'd be missing from home until I could escape from the pound, and who knew how long that would take?

Yes, I was definitely in trouble.

I tried edging backward, putting my stomach down to the ground and looking submissive as all get-out.

Whittenberger kept his gun on me and motioned the deputies around behind me, between me and the house.

Yes, he would definitely shoot me if I tried to run.

I was looking around, wondering just how fast I could move, when I heard something in the alley.

Or rather, I "felt" something.

I "felt" that something was going to happen and that I should be ready.

I also felt very puzzled, but I held myself ready, anyway. It didn't make sense, this "feeling," but neither had anything else that had happened since Sunday evening.

Then there really *was* a noise in the alley. It was like running feet, but not human feet.

The back fence was at least five feet high, but all of a sudden this *thing* came sailing over. It scared me almost as much as the sheriff's gun until I realized that the thing actually looked just like me. The four-footed me, that is. Except that it was a little smaller.

And it didn't land on the ground, it landed on Stanley. Its front feet thumped into his back and sent him sprawling facedown so that he made a very nice landing pad. It didn't waste any time with landing-pad Stanley, however. It immediately launched itself through the air toward Whittenberger. Its open mouth hit his wrist a few inches from the gun he held.

Whittenberger and the gun went flying in opposite directions, the gun hitting the ground and bouncing into the shed through the open door, almost like it had been aimed. The *thing* kept on going, shooting past me at a gallop. It was around the corner of the house before I or anyone else reacted, but as it went past me, I got another of those "feelings," a real humdinger this time.

But at least the feeling matched what I was already planning to do now that Whittenberger's gun wasn't pointed down my throat anymore.

I took off so fast I'm sure I left four pretty deep paw prints in the yard.

Then I was around the corner of the house. I'd forgotten my almost-bundle of clothes during all this, but now I was all of a sudden reminded. The other creature—another werewolf?—was grabbing most of the clothes from under the bush. I had enough sense, now that I'd been reminded, to grab the rest—just my shoes, actually—and then we both ran full tilt out through the front yard and across the street.

Other than wondering who this other werewolf was, my mind was a blank as we ran, although after a couple of minutes the shoes in my mouth started tasting bad. And smelling a little, too, which wasn't all that surprising, considering all the running I'd been doing in them earlier.

After about five minutes, I realized where this other werewolf was leading me.

It was leading me home.

It stopped in the alley behind my house and waited for me to catch up. We looked through the shrubs to the house. There was a light in the living room window, but that was all.

And I was being told—with those "feelings" again—to move quietly.

It led the way, the bundle of clothes still in its mouth, the legs of my trousers dragging on the ground. In a minute, it was under the window to my room.

The window was open.

I hadn't left it open, not tonight!

The other werewolf leaped through. Its claws made hardly a sound, probably because it cleared the windowsill in one, smooth leap.

I followed, somewhat more noisily. First there was the scrabbling on the windowsill and then my shoes hitting the floor as I gratefully dropped them.

My clothes, I saw, had been dropped on the floor at the foot of the bed. The door to the hall was closing softly.

It was crazy, even crazier than being a werewolf who thought he was Spiderman and all that. But somehow I didn't go completely bananas. After all, this *was* a huge improvement over looking down Whittenberger's gun barrel. So I managed to calm myself down enough to change back to human shape and get dressed. Except for my shirt. Two of the buttons had been torn off and one sleeve was ripped. The only damage to the trousers was a slight hole in the cuff and a few damp spots. My wallet—a Christmas present from Mom last year—was still in the back pocket.

I found a good shirt in my closet and I was just putting it on when there was a soft knocking on the door.

"Are you decent yet, Walt?" It was Mom's voice.

"Yes," I said, fastening the last button. I started to kick the torn shirt out of sight under the bed, but I stopped.

"May I come in?" she asked.

"Sure." My voice was a little shaky.

The door opened and she walked in. She was wearing her usual slacks and blouse. Her reddish hair was more mussed than usual, and she looked a little tired. But she was smiling as she looked at me and at the torn shirt.

"You were outgrowing that one anyway," she said.

Which just confirmed it all.

"That was you out there?" I said. I was really surprised how calm I sounded. How calm I really *was*.

She nodded, still smiling. A comforting smile, I guess you'd call it, or maybe an understanding one.

"It runs in the family," she said. "My side of the family, at least."

I didn't say anything. I'm not sure if I was relieved or what. Is being a hereditary werewolf any better than an accidental one? At least this way, you know there are others like you.

"Why?" I asked. "Or maybe I mean, how did it start?"

She shrugged. "I wish I knew. It's been in the family as long as anyone knows." She grinned. "Maybe there really *are* such things as alien shape-changers, and one of them dropped by for a visit a few centuries ago."

"Is Grandma—"

She shook her head. "Not her, your grandfather."

I almost laughed out loud. The idea of a werewolf in a retirement village in Florida struck me funny. It just didn't seem like the right setting. But werewolves have to retire, too, I guess.

"But how did you find me this evening?" I asked. "Were you following me or something?"

"Or something," she said. "Actually, it was partly luck. Your hypnotic friend, Mr. Radsack, called this evening. You remember Mr. Radsack?"

I nodded.

"Well, he wanted to know if the information he'd given you about hypnosis had helped me any. He also said you had asked about hypnotism being able to actually physically change people. It didn't take a great brain to figure out what had happened to you, especially the way you've been acting the last couple of days. I would have warned you about it earlier, except—well, for one thing, I wasn't absolutely sure you had inherited this little family quirk. My brother didn't, for instance. And I wasn't expecting it to show up, even if you *did* have it, for another couple of years. I was sixteen the first time, and your grandfather was seventeen. I guess it must be modern nutrition. Kids just grow up faster these days.

"But when Mr. Radsack called this evening and I realized it had hit you already, I—well, I started 'listening.' Whatever this family quirk is, it gives us some kind of, not communication, really, but *something*. I knew you were getting yourself in trouble, for instance, and I was able to find you. A mental scent or something."

I remembered the vague "feeling" I had had just before she came charging over that fence, and I knew more or less what she meant. It wasn't words or thoughts or pictures or anything else specific like that. Like she said, a "scent," only in my head instead of my nose.

Then I remembered Cindy.

"Someone else knows about me," I said.

"Cindy Deardorf? Mr. Radsack said she was with you when you were asking all your questions."

I nodded. "She was with me the first time it happened, too."

"Since she's still coming around to see you, I assume she didn't panic."

"Hardly. She was calmer than I was."

"You're lucky it was someone like her. There aren't a lot like that." She grinned. "I remember, not long after I started, I really scared a couple of people!"

"They needed it," a new voice said, and I practically jumped out of my skin. "Incidentally, Wilma, I was wondering if you might want to come out of retirement for a good cause? One of the tellers at the bank seems to be developing something of a problem, and—well, the conventional approaches haven't been all that successful. If you could throw a small scare into him . . ."

It was Dad, of course. I just stared at him as he came quietly into the room. My jaw was practically down to my belt buckle.

"Which teller?" Mom asked.

"Pete Wells," he said. "I thought that some evening you might—"

"He knows about you? Us?" I managed to get the words out once I'd gotten my jaw out of my belly button.

"Of course," Mom said. "He's a little like your Cindy, in case you hadn't noticed. Very unflappable and relatively open-minded. Despite a conservative exterior, which does come in rather handy. I mean, who would ever suspect a small-town bank manager of having three werewolves in his immediate family? Even by marriage?"

"But—"

"As I said," she went on, "you don't find many like him. You're lucky you came across Cindy so early."

"I take it," Dad said, "that you were able to get the boy out of whatever scrape he was in?"

Mom made a face. "It was touch and go for a

second, what with Whittenberger and all his deputies, but we made it. Which reminds me," she went on, turning back to me, "what *was* that all about?"

Dad's eyebrows went up. "Deputies? I assume there was a misunderstanding of some kind? After all, I expect my son, werewolf or not, to live up to certain standards."

So I explained about Stanley and the burglaries and everything.

It took quite awhile, and then we spent another few minutes trying to figure out what to do about Stanley, just in case his uncle and the deputies somehow managed to miss the carload of incriminating evidence, even after Mom had knocked the sheriff's gun right into the shed. We hadn't come up with anything really brilliant when the doorbell rang and someone started banging like he wanted to knock the whole door down.

A quick glance out the window showed us it was Cindy. A truck was sitting at the curb directly in front of the house, idling.

I looked at Mom a little worriedly. "Is it okay if I tell her about you?"

"I assumed you'd probably have to. She must have heard how you were rescued, and she will no doubt want to know who the second werewolf was. Won't she?"

''Definitely,'' I said.

And Cindy did, of course, want to know, which is sort of like saying ''Hitler wasn't really a very nice person.'' She was practically breaking out in curiosity hives when I finally opened the door.

The truck, its driver waving an anonymous arm out the window, pulled away when the door opened. ''Who—'' I began, but that was as far as I got.

''The man from the bottle booth,'' Cindy said. ''He wanted to make sure things went okay at Willard's, and he let me ride along with him. Then when we were sure they were really going to arrest Stanley no matter *what* his uncle said, he gave me a ride here, and everyone back there said there were *two* weird-looking dogs, and I supposed one of them was you, but who was—''

That's when she saw Mom standing in the hall just behind me, and her mouth closed so fast her teeth clicked.

''It's okay,'' I said. ''Mom knows all about it. And Dad.''

Her eyes widened, and I thought for a second she was really going to panic. ''You really *are* all alien shapechangers!'' she said in a whisper.

''Not that I know of,'' I said, ''and besides, it's just Mom.''

"Oh." Cindy blinked a couple of times and finally came inside.

And we explained it all to her. As much as we knew, anyway.

And Cindy took it very well, which didn't surprise me. She'd had plenty of practice in taking things well recently. Besides, like she said once she had gotten used to the idea, "Why should three werewolves in a family be any harder to believe than one? Anyway, it was probably easier to become one back then."

And that's about it, except for Stanley's trial, which will be coming up in a few weeks, and Cindy's idea. Tim and Willard are both going to testify against him, so Cindy and I won't have to do anything more. As for Cindy's idea . . .

It popped out when I told her about the job offer from the two Sevastopol Simians who'd been so impressed with my "wolf trick," and she's been bugging me about it ever since. I'm not sure how much longer I can hold out against all her hints, orders, etc., to "learn how to bang the cymbals or *something!*"

Her idea is that the two of us could be a "package." The Simians could hire me for my "wolf trick," but they'd have to take Cindy, too, as a singer. I think she's even got ideas of starting her

own group in a few years. I know she's got a song all written. A theme song, I guess, called "The Ballad of Werewolf Walt," which she would expect me to demonstrate while she did the singing.

Dad's a little dubious. He figures it might get out of control sometime. "Scaring one of my tellers into solving his problem is one thing, but getting up on a stage in front of hundreds of people . . ."

But Mom sounds like she's on Cindy's side. "Just be sure you finish school first" is about the only caution she ever gives me. "Even werewolves need an education." That and "Always make the change in a lot of smoke so no one will ever start thinking your 'wolf trick' is for real."

So I guess I don't really have a chance, and besides, it *does* sound like it could be fun. With Cindy, anyway. With her, almost anything is fun.

Besides, as Mom sometimes says with a small smile, "This *is* the first really practical use our family has put the werewolf business to in at least the last four generations."